Melanie took her aunt's frail hand in hers. "Aunt Sarah," she said huskily. "I was so scared. How do you feel?"

"Don't you worry about me, Melly girl. I'm just relieved to see you safe."

Melanie gave Lieutenant Tucker a startled glance. Her confusion was mirrored on his face.

"Mrs. Swanson, why wouldn't your niece be safe?"

Sarah narrowed her eyes at him. Mel could almost feel her aunt's distrust. After all, he had led her niece away in handcuffs all those years ago.

Now was not the time, though, to harbor grudges.

"Aunt Sarah, if something's going on, you have to tell Lieutenant Tucker," she insisted.

"Melly, one of the jurors came to see me," Sarah whispered. "She was so scared. Said that she had received threats during the trial."

Lieutenant Tucker stepped closer. "What kind of threats?"

"She was told to vote guilty or else. The young woman said that her conscience was killing her. I think she was worried that whoever wanted you in prison so bad would come after you now that you were free."

Melanie felt the horror sink into her soul. Would this never end? All she wanted was to try to put her life back together. Somehow, she had found herself in the middle of something dark.

Something deadly.

Dana R. Lynn grew up in Illinois. She met her husband at a wedding and told her parents she had met her future husband. Nineteen months later, they were married. Today, they live in rural Pennsylvania with their three children and enough pets to open a petting zoo. In addition to writing, she works as an educational interpreter for the deaf and is active in several ministries at her church.

Books by Dana R. Lynn

Love Inspired Suspense

Presumed Guilty

PRESUMED GUILTY

DANA R. LYNN

HARLEQUIN® LOVE INSPIRED® SUSPENSE

Recycling programs for this product may not exist in your area.

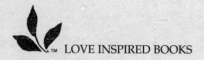

™ LOVE INSPIRED BOOKS

ISBN-13: 978-0-373-44664-3

Presumed Guilty

www.Harlequin.com

Printed in U.S.A.

Trust in the Lord with all your heart; and lean not unto your own understanding. In all your ways acknowledge Him and He will direct your paths.
—*Proverbs* 3:5-6

This book is dedicated to the memory
of my father and my brother, Greg. Miss you.

To my husband, Brad, and my children—I love you so much!
You are my greatest blessing.

To my Lord and Savior,
I hope my life always gives You glory.

Acknowledgments

So many people to thank!

To my mom, my brothers and my huge extended family...
I can't believe all the support. Thanks!

To my amazing editor at Love Inspired Suspense,
Elizabeth Mazer... Thank you for this awesome opportunity.
Your guidance has been invaluable. I hope to work with you
for many years to come. Yay, Team Elizabeth!

To my agent, Mary Sue Seymour... Thank you for taking a
chance on me. I appreciate all you do on my behalf.

To my best friends/prayer warriors, Amy and Dee...
What would I do without you guys? Love you!

To my critique partners, Christina, Erica and Rhonda...
I couldn't have done this without you ladies.

ONE

"There she is!"

"Melanie, can you give us a statement? How does it feel to be released? Do you still claim to be innocent?"

"She's a murderer! She should still be rotting in jail!" Prying questions, angry jeers and insults assailed Melanie's ears. She kept her head turned away from the mob standing behind the police officers stationed near the road. She had hoped the combination of the brisk March wind and the early hour would keep the vultures away. No such luck. Her heel slipped on a patch of black ice left over from winter. The ghost of a malicious chuckle reached her ear. She steadied herself, trembling.

A rock sailed through the air. It struck her pale cheek. She could feel blood well and drip down her face. She refused to brush it away, to allow them the satisfaction of seeing that she was hurt.

Wow. She was being stoned in public and no one seemed to care. If anything, the sight of her blood seemed to inflame them. The shouts grew louder, and someone started chanting, "Murderer! Murderer!" The crowd picked up the chant. It sent ice down Melanie's spine.

A muscled arm shot in front of her face, deflecting a second rock. The owner of the arm placed a strong hand on her shoulder. Not in comfort, but in an attempt to keep her moving. She didn't acknowledge him. She already knew that Lieutenant Jace Tucker agreed with the crowd.

"Officers, control those people!" he barked into the radio fastened to his shoulder.

Mel shuddered as Lieutenant Tucker's harsh voice washed over her.

Without warning, a swarm of hungry reporters closed in on her, threatening to swallow her whole. She ducked her head to avoid the cameras flashing around her. The cacophony of voices surrounding her was deafening, one voice melting into the next. At least the hooded sweatshirt she was wearing allowed her to hide part of her face. Hopefully, her bleeding cheek wouldn't make the evening news.

"Melanie, Senator Travis was quoted yesterday as saying you should have served more time for the death of Sylvie Walters. Any comment? Have you talked to his son, your fiancé?"

Ex-fiancé.

Not for the first time, Melanie struggled against bitterness toward the senator, who had used her court case as his own political platform to be harsh on crime. It wouldn't surprise her to find out he was responsible for this mob.

Melanie kept her face blank, but her chest tightened. One trembling hand slipped into her jeans pocket and closed around her inhaler. *Please Lord, let me make it to the car.*

One intrepid soul darted past her police escort and thrust a microphone into Mel's startled face. "Come on, Melanie. You were in prison for almost four years after being convicted of manslaughter. Surely there's something you'd like to say. A message for Sylvie's family, maybe?"

The callous remark slammed into her, robbing her of her breath.

"No comment, people. Give us room."

Against her will, Melanie glanced to her left to take in the man walking beside her. Lieutenant Tucker met her eyes briefly, his own as hard as flint, his face an inscrutable mask.

Why was he here? Couldn't they have found someone else for this duty—someone who wouldn't look at her with such clear disdain? Her knees trembled as he moved beside her. She resisted the urge to step away from him. Jerking her eyes forward, she strove to act as though he weren't there. But his image had been seared into her mind.

Strong. Determined. A man of faith. And the man who had personally slapped handcuffs on her and coldly recited her Miranda rights. And now she had to sedately walk by his side as if her heart weren't pounding and her insides quaking. *Pull yourself together, Mel,* she ordered herself sternly. *All you have to do is make it to Aunt Sarah's house. Then you never have to set eyes on his odious face again.* Okay, so maybe *odious* was a bit too strong a word. Still, she didn't think she would be too upset when he was out of her life for good.

She flicked a nervous glance at the stony-faced man beside her, shivering at the utter coldness in his deep blue eyes. His short blond hair was the color of wheat ripe for the harvest. His strong jaw was clenched as he walked by her side, emphasizing the distaste he felt for this assignment.

Well, that was too bad. She straightened her shoulders. Directly ahead, she could see the police cruiser waiting. All she needed to do was get through the gauntlet of reporters and angry protestors.

One of the protestors suddenly thrust himself forward. He planted himself in her way, ignoring the fierce scowl on Lieutenant Tucker's face. Stabbing a threatening finger at her, the demonstrator leaned in until he was almost touching her. Anger spilled from his eyes. His pungent breath fanned her face. Mel stumbled back. Only the Lieutenant's iron grip on her arm kept her from falling. As soon as she had her balance, he released her. Fast. As if just touching her would contaminate him. Humiliated, she tried to walk around the man in front of her.

"You think you'll get away with this, don't you? Like father, like daughter." He sneered. "That poor girl's dead, and you go free after just a few measly years inside. But you'll never be free. We're watching you. We won't forget. You will pay the way you deserve, one way or another."

Melanie's stomach turned at the mention of her father and at the menace in the man's tone.

"Move along, mister, or you'll find yourself arrested for threatening her," Lieutenant Tucker ordered.

Not that he disagrees, Mel thought. Oh, she doubted the Lieutenant was the type to resort to vigilante justice, but it was clear he thought prison was exactly where she belonged. Despair welled up inside her. She clamped down on her emotions. No way was she going to show any hint of vulnerability. Not in front of these vultures. Her face a stoic mask, she let herself into the passenger's side of the police cruiser. Her hands gripped together in her lap as she waited for Lieutenant Tucker to join her.

He slammed the driver's side door and started the car, muttering to himself. She waited until he had driven away from the crowd before taking her inhaler out and using it. She almost cried with relief as her inflamed air passages opened, allowing her to breathe freely. Lieutenant Tucker darted wary glances her way.

"Are you all right?" he asked her, his tone of voice suggesting he was only asking because he felt obligated to do so.

"I'm fine. Thank you for agreeing to drive me home."

He threw a furious scowl her way. "Yeah," he retorted, sarcasm heavy in his voice, "this is exactly what I wanted to be doing today."

"I'm sor—" She halted. No way would she apologize for any of this. Whether he believed it or not, she was the victim, and had been for a long time. Fueled by indignation, she found her anger and became bold. "Why are you even here? It's obvious you agree with those nuts out there."

His eyes widened, but were just as quickly shuttered. Had she surprised him with her candor?

"It's my job. My boss felt you were in danger. Whether or not I agree, the chief wanted someone here. I drew the short straw. So here I am…a glorified babysitter for an ex-con."

That hurt. Melanie looked out the window as frustration clawed at her throat, making her voice tight when she spoke.

"I am not a criminal."

"A jury of your peers disagreed."

"I don't care." Her voice was low and husky. "I never sold drugs to anyone, especially not to teenagers."

He sighed and rolled his eyes. "Sure, sure. You were just a victim of circumstances."

"I was!"

"Look, lady…"

"My name is Melanie, not Lady."

"Whatever. The point is, *Melanie*, no matter how innocent you claim to be, all the evidence implicated you. I collected it myself."

"I know," Melanie responded bitterly. "But it was all circumstantial. What absolute proof was there?"

The lieutenant made a disgusted sound. "If you were so innocent, why the suicide attempt?"

Distress filled Melanie. An inarticulate sound of pain escaped from her throat, almost like that of a wounded animal. "I didn't… I wouldn't…" she choked out, and turned to face the window. This time, the tears would not be held back. They trickled in a slow stream down her cheek.

She heard him sigh again but was determined to ignore him. Awful man. How dare he treat her this way? Even if she had been guilty, she had served her sentence and paid her debt to society. She knew in her heart, though, that she was not guilty. Proving it, however, had been beyond her power. Maybe if she could have remembered the night in question…she shook her head. She needed to move on.

"Melanie."

She refused to acknowledge him.

"Melanie, I'm sorry." The words sounded somewhat strangled.

She turned around from the window and glared at him. "Don't choke on your apology."

Unexpectedly, he chuckled. A shiver went down her spine at the pleasant sound. Under different circumstances, she might have been attracted to him. As it was, she couldn't help but view him as an adversary.

"I won't say that I don't think you're guilty, because I do." Melanie turned away from him. "I will apologize for my unprofessional behavior."

She nodded in acknowledgment. What else could she say?

The remainder of the thirty-minute drive from Erie to LaMar Pond was silent. Uncomfortable. Melanie kept her gaze fixed on the passing scenery outside her window. *Only a few more minutes,* she told herself when she saw the sign for LaMar Pond. The car slowed as the lieutenant maneuvered past two Amish buggies. Lieutenant Tucker and Melanie both sighed in relief when her aunt's house came into view. It would have been humorous if the circumstances had been different.

Dear Aunt Sarah. Even with all the supposed "evidence," she had refused to believe her only niece could have committed the vile acts of which she was accused. Everyone else abandoned Mel. Her friends, her coworkers at the restaurant, even her fiancé. But not Aunt Sarah. For that alone, Melanie would be forever grateful.

The cruiser turned onto the gravel path that led up to the small cottage Sarah Swanson had built with her husband thirty years earlier. The area remained remarkably untouched in the years that followed. The closest neighbor was half a mile away. Melanie had always loved the peacefulness. The lack of people around appealed to her. Especially now. Impatience grabbed her. She tried to open her door. Locked. Throwing Lieutenant Tucker a scowl, she gestured toward the door. He rolled his eyes as he unlocked it. Ignoring him, she pushed the door open and ran up the front steps.

She stopped. Uneasiness shivered through her. The front door was open. Aunt Sarah never left doors open.

"What's the holdup?"

She whirled to face the grim-faced man stalking toward her.

"Lieutenant," she started. Stopped. If she shared her suspicions, he would think she was playing games. Her aunt had probably felt tired and left the door open so her niece wouldn't have to wait for her to maneuver through the house in her wheelchair. Mel remembered how drama wore her aunt out.

Melanie flattened her mouth into a determined line. Straightening her shoulders, she pushed the door open and entered. And screamed.

* * *

Melanie's scream pushed Jace into action. He bolted up the stairs. He found Melanie kneeling on the floor beside her aunt's unconscious body. Tears streamed down her face. She was shaking her aunt's shoulder and calling her name. No response. Jace glanced around, his eyes alert. Sarah's chair was still where it had been when she fell out of it. A shattered mug was on the floor. Sarah herself was lying in a puddle of what looked like hot chocolate. Her wispy white curls were matted with the liquid.

Instinctively, Jace fell back on his first-aid training. He glanced around the room, making sure no other dangers lurked before falling to his knees beside Melanie. He could hear the elderly woman's labored breathing. Together, they carefully turned her onto her back. Melanie gasped at the sight, and Jace could hardly blame her. Sarah Swanson's eyelids and lips were swollen to three times their normal size.

"Anaphylactic shock?" Jace queried.

Mel nodded in agreement. She raced to the desk against the wall and tore open her aunt's purse, desperately riffling through its contents.

"Yes!" Triumphantly, Mel held up the object she had been searching for. An EpiPen. Jace made room for her as she rushed back. Throwing herself on her knees next to the prone woman, she jabbed the needle into her aunt's thigh. Then she sat back on her heels. Jace watched the desperation leave her face as her aunt's breathing became more natural. Holding Melanie's eyes, he flipped open his phone and called for an ambulance. Releasing her gaze, he stood. He needed to call the chief and give him an update.

Smash!

Mel screamed again. The brick that had been flung through the window landed with a *thud* beside her. Glass shards glistened in her hair. In the midmorning sunlight, they resembled diamonds.

Jace barked a request for backup into the radio clipped to his shoulder. He raced to the window. His gun seemed to jump into his hand. He peered outside, squinting as he examined the thick line of trees surrounding the cottage. Nothing moved. A quick glance down, though, showed fresh footprints in the flower bed below the window. Large footprints. Whoever had thrown that rock was probably around six feet tall. Jace figured the person was in shape given how fast they escaped the scene. In the distance, an engine roared to life. Jace let out a frustrated sigh as he realized pursuit would be pointless.

A gasp behind him caused him to whirl. Melanie was staring at a crinkled piece of paper. She was trying to keep it steady, but her hands shook violently. Her face was ashen. She looked as though she might faint. Alarmed, Jace went to her and snatched the paper out of her grasp. She didn't even flinch.

MURDERER! YOU ARE NOT WELCOME HERE. LEAVE WHILE YOU CAN.

The large block letters had been cut out of magazines and newspapers. Whoever had thrown that rock made sure their handwriting couldn't be traced. That amount of effort pointed to premeditation. The person had probably been outside the window waiting for Melanie's return.

Jace scowled. What kind of lowlife threatened women? Sarah Swanson was about as harmless as you could get. And as for Melanie… He narrowed his eyes as he gazed at the young woman. Her face was pale, and her lips seemed bloodless. The dark curls framing her face emphasized the pallor. The haunted look in her velvet brown eyes tore at him. Even knowing her past as he did, Jace disliked seeing her slender frame tremble with fear.

He hated himself for feeling drawn to her. He thought he had banished the attraction four years ago. A flare of resentment surged as he looked at the young woman kneeling on the floor. Hadn't he learned his lesson? He had let affection cloud his judgment once before, with disastrous results. Never again.

Melanie raised her head. Her eyes met his. His hair stood on end as electricity zapped between them. Then, as if a light had been switched off, Melanie's eyes became guarded. He could see her exercising every bit of control she had to master her fear and appear calm. She was brave. He'd give her that. He would have expected tears or outright panic. He wasn't about to complain, though. Having a hysterical woman on his hands would only make a bad situation worse.

To distract himself, he turned his attention to Sarah Swanson. She was still unconscious, but the swelling around her mouth and eyes was noticeably diminished. He could see that her chest was moving now as she breathed, a sure sign that she was improved.

Jace cleared his throat. "I need to look around outside. Stay by your aunt. Yell if you see any changes."

"Should I clean up the glass? So the paramedics don't step in it?"

"Leave it. I called for another cruiser. We need to process the scene first. I'll make sure it's cleaned up afterward."

Zipping his coat, he strode toward the door, noticing they had left it wide-open in the excitement. He spent the next ten minutes searching for evidence. Other than footprints that led off into the woods, he found nothing. A horn honked. He lifted a hand in greeting as another cruiser pulled in, followed by the paramedics. A third cruiser pulled in and parked in the yard. Jace raised his eyebrows. A third cruiser was unusual, to say the least.

He led the paramedics into the house and set the two officers about evaluating the scene. One of the officers approached Melanie. Jace stiffened. It was natural to question her, but the look of attraction on the officer's face was unsettling. They were cops. It was their duty to remain focused. Letting an ex-con, no matter how pretty, distract them was not going to happen. Jace made his voice stern.

"Olsen, go help Jacobs. I'll want your report ASAP."

"Yes, sir." The young policeman cast one last regretful glance at Melanie and returned outside.

"On three…" The paramedics lifted Sarah Swanson onto a stretcher and loaded her into the ambulance.

Mel looked around the room, feeling lost. Her aunt was on her way to the hospital, and no one would talk to her or tell her what she should do. It was disconcerting enough being out of jail, away from the routines that had, for better or for worse, been her life for the past four years. She'd been told that she'd have to adjust to life on the "outside," but no one had explained how to deal with something like this. How was she going to get to the hospital? Was she supposed to go in the ambulance? Would someone drive her? Should she get a taxi? Unthinkingly, her eyes sought out the lieutenant. He might not like her, but he was the only steadying presence in the house.

Melanie glanced at him again. He had just flipped his phone shut and was talking with the officers as the ambulance roared to life and headed back to town toward the hospital. Well, that answered one question. Since no one was paying attention to her, Melanie made her way to her old bedroom.

Melanie stood in the doorway, breathing deeply. The

room was the same as it had been nine years ago when she moved out. The blue-and-lavender color scheme, the ruffled curtains. Even the Bible her aunt had given her on her seventeenth birthday was there, sitting on the little end table beside the bed. Waiting for her. Mel walked over and picked the Bible up. Tears clogged her throat.

She had sneered at that Bible when she had received it, she remembered now with pain. What would she need that for? she had scoffed. Her aunt had merely smiled sadly.

"Someday, Melly," Aunt Sarah had replied softly, "someday you'll need a friend. Someone strong to carry you. This is where you'll find Him."

Her younger self had rolled her eyes at her aunt's "preaching." Thinking about it now, Mel was pretty sure she had never opened it. She didn't even know why she had kept it. It wasn't that she'd wanted to protect her aunt's feelings. If that had been the case, she wouldn't have walked out the moment she graduated from high school nine years ago.

But she had never gotten rid of it. And when she moved out, her aunt had left it here as if she had known that someday her wayward niece would come back for it. Although neither of them could ever have guessed that it would take a prison sentence to bring Mel to God.

Sitting on the bed, she opened the Bible to the book of Psalms. She read slowly, until she felt peace seep into her soul. Feeling calm again, she closed the Bible and stood. She startled when she saw Lieutenant Tucker standing in the doorway. He watched her, his brow furrowed and the corners of his lips pulled down.

She walked over to him and waited.

He stared back for several seconds. Then he straightened and nodded.

"Right," he said briskly. "Let's go. I'll take you to the hospital."

Mel hesitated. She didn't relish the idea of remaining in his presence any longer than she needed to. He had made his disdain known. He was a man who viewed her as a criminal, and always would. Even if she could find a way to prove her innocence, would he believe it? Or was he too hardened against her?

Lieutenant Tucker frowned at her hesitation. "Come on, Melanie. I really don't have all day."

Melanie shivered at the chill in Lieutenant Tucker's deep voice. His contempt for her was almost tangible. The last thing she wanted to do was get back into the cruiser with him. She needed to go to Aunt Sarah, though, so she followed him to the car.

As he backed down the driveway, she caught one last glance of the house. A shudder ran through her as the sunlight glinted off the broken window. She had been released from the horrors of prison only to walk into a new nightmare.

TWO

The scenery sped past as Jace drove to the hospital. Melanie tried to ask a question or two. He only grunted in reply. He couldn't talk now. His mind was busy analyzing what had happened. The scene at the house made him uneasy.

She seemed to get the message. The silence settled around them like a cloak.

Jace couldn't accept that the events of the day were all coincidental. Too much had happened in less than two hours.

Melanie had been released from prison.

She had been verbally threatened by the man in front of the courthouse.

Sarah Swanson had been found comatose.

Someone had thrown a rock through the window.

Jace had found Melanie reading her Bible.

That had really thrown him for a loop. Against his better judgment, he found himself feeling sympathy for the pretty brunette. The distress in her brown eyes over her aunt's condition was real, he was sure of it. He had gone searching for her, knowing she would need a ride to the hospital. He watched in disbelief as she leafed through the Bible. Not idly. Purposefully, as though she knew what she was looking for. When she had finally noticed him, the expression of peace on her face shook him.

"I don't understand what happened to Aunt Sarah." Melanie's voice interrupted his musings. He threw her a confused frown.

"I assumed she was stung by a bee."

She shook her head. "The only thing she's allergic to is peanuts. She's always been extremely careful. She would never eat or drink anything without reading its ingredient list." Mel shifted her position and narrowed her eyes, looking as though she was speaking out loud to help her think. "She was so careful I used to tell her she went overboard. Nothing was ever in her house that had even been processed in the same factory with peanuts. If she needed to special-order items she would. No. I just can't imagine her accidentally eating something with peanuts or peanut oil in it."

He wasn't sure why, but Jace believed her. Jace had learned long ago to trust his instincts. He was uneasy. If Sarah had not ingested something tainted by accident, then it had been placed there deliberately. The question reverberating around his mind was who would do such a thing.

He parked the car, and they strode into the hospital. Jace caught Melanie's elbow as they crossed the wet parking lot. She gave him a startled glance.

"It's slippery out here," he explained defensively. Yeah, right.

She quirked her eyebrow but said nothing.

They hadn't gone more than a dozen steps when a voice called out to them. Jace tried to ignore the speaker, but it was too late. Of course he would have to run into Senator Travis now. He shouldn't have been surprised. Mrs. Travis had been in the hospital for over a week now. It was only natural that her husband would visit her. Still, the timing was lousy. Not that any time would be convenient. Senator Travis had rubbed him the wrong way since he had been elected to the state senate. He was rude and arrogant, and Jace had noted that he had broken many of his campaign promises within months of getting elected. In Jace's mind, that showed a lack of integrity.

"Lieutenant Tucker! I need a moment of your time!"

Resigned, Jace motioned for Melanie to stop.

"Wait here. I'll be as quick as I can."

He made his way over to where Senator Joe Travis was waiting impatiently. The senator's eyes slid past him and landed on Melanie. Jace's spine stiffened in annoyance when the older man's lips curled in a derisive sneer.

"Looks like you got short straw today, son, escorting the likes of her around town."

Jace refused to comment. However he might feel about it, it was his duty, and he would do it without complaint.

"You wanted to talk with me, Senator Travis?"

The senator whipped his face back around to glare at Jace.

"I want to know when you're going to get around to doing your duty. Someone broke into my house last night!" The senator seemed to swell with righteous anger.

"Was anything taken?"

The man hesitated. "Nothing really valuable. A few things here and there. Some pictures. Some of my wife's jewels."

"Not all of her jewels?"

"No. The thief left some of the older pieces that my wife inherited from her mother. Must not have known how valuable they are."

"Okay, here's what you need to do. Go to the station and file a report, listing the items stolen and their approximate value. Be as specific as you can." Jace bit back a smile. Senator Travis practically vibrated with frustration.

"You can't take my statement now? I'm a very busy man!" The senator narrowed his eyes, a sly expression creeping onto his face. "Or are you letting our local ex-con charm her way into your life? Be careful, she's a clever one. Good thing my son came to his senses."

Any thought Jace might have had of helping the man fled. The implication that he would be so easily manipulated, that he lacked the sense and the willpower to maintain control over himself, was more insulting than the senator could have realized. And it triggered painful memories that he did not care to revisit. Ever.

"Sorry, sir. No time today." Before the senator could respond, he swiftly headed back to where Melanie was waiting with a wary expression. Without slowing, he grabbed her arm above the elbow and pulled her along with him.

"Don't look back. Whatever you do, don't look back. He might come after us."

"Okay, I won't look," Melanie assured him, gasping as she was dragged to the hospital entrance.

Once inside, they were directed to the waiting room. Jace pretended to read the newspaper as he sat. In reality, he watched Melanie. She was staring out the window, her eyes slightly unfocused. The light coming in caught in her hair, giving off reddish highlights. There were still a few shards of glass there, glistening. He had the urge to walk over and pick them out. Her porcelain-smooth complexion was marred only by the pensive line on her brow. Until she turned her head slightly and the light fell on an inch-long cut. He remembered the rock that had been thrown at her earlier. It had been his duty to protect her. He had failed.

She hardly seemed aware of the cut. Every expression, every gesture, showed nothing but anxiety over her aunt.

Gazing at her and seeing how worried she was, remembering how she had turned to the Bible for consolation, he found it incredible that she was capable of the crimes she had been accused of. Doubt slithered across his mind. He quickly shoved it aside. The evidence had been there. True, it was mostly circumstantial. There were no DNA matches, no incriminating fingerprints. But he knew from experience that an appealing face and charming manners could be deceptive.

Jace shook his head fiercely. He refused to second-guess himself. If he did, he would go insane. So she had been careful at the scene. But she had been there when Sylvie died. She couldn't deny that fact, even if she couldn't remember exactly what had happened that day. Melanie had admitted that she and Sylvie planned to meet at the dorm the day of the younger girl's death. According to Melanie's testimony, she didn't know why Sylvie had contacted her, asking to meet. Sylvie was a freshman, and Melanie, at twenty-one, was in her last semester of the dental hygienist program. The two had no overlap in their coursework or in their friends, no reason to be in contact—except for the drugs that Sylvie took and that they had every reason to believe Melanie sold her. Tainted drugs that killed Sylvie and left Melanie responsible for her death. Eyes narrowing, he resumed his observance of his charge.

Melanie leaned her head against the cold window and closed her eyes. He saw her sigh, then her lips began moving. It was almost as though she was talking, but not a sound issued from her mouth. Could she be praying? As much as he wanted to scoff at the idea, the memory of her sitting reading her Bible was firmly implanted in his brain. It couldn't have been staged. She had no way of knowing he would come searching for her. And the Bible had looked far too natural in her hands.

Melanie opened her eyes and turned her head. Their eyes met, and all thoughts fled. He could feel the electricity sparking between them.

"Lieutenant Tucker? Miss Swanson?"

Both occupants in the waiting room startled.

A doctor stood in the doorway. He glanced between them, a serious expression on his lined face.

Jace quickly rose to his feet. Melanie, he noticed, watched the doctor almost fearfully. Her aunt was all she had, Jace realized. A rush of sympathy unexpectedly filled him. When she stepped next to him, he reached out and squeezed her hand briefly before dropping it again. Blood heated his face as she looked at him, shocked. What on earth had come over him? He took a step away from her.

The doctor cleared his throat.

"I'm Dr. Jensen, the physician in charge of Mrs. Swanson's care. Mrs. Swanson has regained consciousness," he informed them. Melanie's shoulders sagged as the tension melted from her. Tears filled her eyes. "She's groggy, and we'll need to observe her overnight. She is asking to see you."

Melanie fought back tears as she gazed down at her aunt's withered frame. The years had not been kind to her. Melanie remembered how strong she had seemed to Melanie when she was a child. How old she appeared now! Her once-thick white hair had thinned, leaving patches of scalp visible. Her face was gaunt, the skin stretched taut against her high cheekbones. Her eyes were sunken into the sockets. Her aunt's whole body appeared fragile. The robust woman who had raised her since her mother's death had completely disappeared. Melanie knew most of the changes in her aunt were due to the stress of Melanie's arrest. The reddened lids lifted, and Mel found herself staring into sharp blue eyes.

"Mel," the old woman whispered, her voice crackling like dry leaves.

Melanie swallowed. She had come so close to losing this dear woman. Reaching out, she took her aunt's frail hand in hers.

"Aunt Sarah," she said huskily. "I was so scared. How do you feel?"

"Don't you worry about me, Melly girl. I'm just relieved to see you safe."

Melanie gave Lieutenant Tucker a startled glance. Her confusion was mirrored on his face.

"What do you mean, Mrs. Swanson? Why wouldn't your niece be safe?"

Sarah Swanson narrowed her eyes at him. Mel could almost feel her aunt's distrust. Not that she could blame her. After all, he had led her niece away in handcuffs all those years ago.

Now was not the time, though, to harbor grudges.

"Aunt Sarah, if something's going on, you have to tell Lieutenant Tucker," she insisted. "There's more at stake here than my reputation."

The lieutenant nodded. "Melanie's right. I need to know what's going on."

"Melly, one of the jurors came to see me," Sarah whispered. "She was so scared. Terrified. Said that she and at least one of the other jurors had received threatening phone calls and letters during the trial."

"Threats?" Lieutenant Tucker stepped closer. "What kind of threats?"

Sarah coughed and closed her eyes. "They were told to vote guilty or else. The young woman, Alayna Brown,

I think, was worried that whoever it was would go after her parents."

"Aunt Sarah." Melanie kept her voice soft, soothing. "You said another juror was threatened, too. Do you know who? Did she say?"

"No, dear." The old woman opened her eyes and pierced Melanie with her gaze. "She said that her conscience was killing her. She was afraid that she'd helped to jail an innocent woman and keep a killer free. I think she was worried that whoever wanted you in prison so bad would come after you now that you were free."

Melanie felt the horror sink into her soul. Would this never end? All she wanted was to try to put her life back together. Somehow, she had found herself in the middle of something dark.

Something deadly.

A footstep stopped outside the door. Melanie frowned, and craned her neck to see who was at the door. When she saw the empty doorway, she shook her head. Great. Now she was hearing things.

"Mrs. Swanson," Lieutenant Tucker addressed her aunt gently, "I'm going to ask for someone to guard your door during your stay. I'll do my best to find out who's behind this. Please trust me."

"Melly," the old lady wheezed urgently.

"I'll protect her, Mrs. Swanson. With my life if necessary." He leaned over and placed a hand over Sarah's. When he straightened, he took out his phone and motioned to Melanie that he was going to be right outside the door. She nodded her understanding. She tried to focus her attention on her aunt, but found herself listening in on the lieutenant's side of the conversation.

"Sir, I know we have limited resources. There needs

to be someone here with the aunt. Yes, sir. I believe she's in danger."

Melanie's throat constricted. Poor Aunt Sarah! She had never done anyone harm, and now she had been targeted. Melanie knew this whole mess was her fault.

"I can keep an eye on the niece. We just need cover for the aunt."

Her face heated at the idea of spending so much time with the irritating lieutenant. She remembered his look of contempt back at the house. He didn't even care that she insisted she was innocent. Even if she had been guilty, she wasn't the same woman who went to jail four years ago. Not that Lieutenant Tucker would ever believe her.

"Melanie, child." Aunt Sarah's whispery voice broke into her reverie.

"Yes, Aunt Sarah?"

"Sing for me. Please. It's been so long since I heard you sing."

Melanie's breathing hitched. She had forgotten how much her aunt had loved to listen to her. Deliberately, she chose a French aria that she knew her aunt loved. As she sang, she allowed her eyes to close, losing herself in the music. When she opened them again, her gaze was caught by a pair of blue eyes. Lieutenant Tucker had returned, and was staring at her with his jaw dropped.

Embarrassed, she rose awkwardly to her feet.

Lieutenant Tucker straightened and nodded. "Let's go."

With a grimace, Melanie said goodbye to Aunt Sarah, promising to visit again soon, and then followed him out. She hadn't realized how tall he was. But now, trying to keep up with his long strides, she realized he was a good eight or nine inches taller than her own five feet four inches. By the time they had reached the parking lot, she was almost jogging to keep up. What was his hurry? She didn't remember him walking so fast earlier.

Irritated, she stopped. She planted her fists firmly on her slim hips. And waited.

Lieutenant Tucker was about twenty feet ahead of her when he slowed and glanced around. His expression grew as dark as a thundercloud. He fixed the fiercest glare Melanie had ever seen on her, and she resisted the urge to take a step back. Instead, she lifted her chin, and gave him what she hoped was a defiant scowl.

"What are you playing at, Melanie?" he demanded.

"I'm not going to run after you," she tossed back at him. "My legs are shorter than yours."

He huffed. "Of all the—"

A sudden squeal of tires cut off whatever he was about to say. A dark four-door sedan came barreling around the corner of the parking lot. It was headed right for her!

Melanie stood, frozen, filled with the certainty that she was going to die.

Lieutenant Tucker rammed into her with enough force to send her flying six feet before she slammed into the pavement. She lay still for a couple of seconds before sitting up, wincing. The lieutenant was already calling the incident in on the radio clipped to his shoulder. He didn't get a good look at the license plate, she heard him say.

"We need to look over the security tapes before we leave," he informed her. "Whoever that was almost killed us with their recklessness. There's no excuse for accidents like that to happen."

Melanie was silent. Part of her wondered if it really had been an accident.

"Do we know where we're going?" Mel inquired. They had been driving in silence for ten minutes.

"Of course I know," Lieutenant Tucker replied, his expression bordering on smug. After a few seconds, Mel realized he wasn't planning on saying anything more.

"Well, could you tell me where?"

"I could. Don't know why I should, though. You're a civilian."

Mel sputtered in confusion. "Well, because… Jace!" She nearly yelled the last as she caught his satisfied smirk. Then her face reddened as she realized she had slipped up and called him by his first name. "I mean Lieutenant."

"Jace is fine."

She gave him her most mutinous glare.

He relented. "Fine. *We're* going to an apartment complex on Sassafras Street. That's Alayna Brown's last known address."

Startled, Melanie couldn't help asking, "You mean you're going to let me talk to her?"

He shrugged. "Why wouldn't I?"

"Well," Melanie said, "if you're investigating the threats—which you are, right?" Jace nodded. "Then is it okay for me to be there? I mean, it's not like I'm a police officer."

Jace's derisive snort in response irritated her, but she stayed quiet, waiting for him to answer. "You're right that I usually wouldn't bring a civilian along while I went to take someone's statement," he said at last. "But these are unusual circumstances. You seem to be in danger. I promised my chief I would look after you. I have to question Alayna, and I can't leave you unsupervised, which means you have to go where I go. And anyway, your aunt said that Alayna was worried about you. She might be more willing to talk if you're there."

Satisfied, and more than a little apprehensive, Melanie

sat back and allowed the silence to swallow them as Jace turned off the interstate and headed toward the city limits.

"Your voice is incredible."

Taken aback, her eyes swiveled back to Jace. His expression clearly said he hadn't meant to tell her that. In fact, he refused to glance her way.

"Thank you." Really, what else was there to say?

"That was an unusual song choice."

Jace apparently hated mysteries of any kind.

"My aunt has loved that song forever. I grew up listening to it. It only made sense to learn to sing it." She shrugged. She had never really given thought to her talent. It was just something she enjoyed doing. Truth be known, she often found herself singing without being aware of it. That habit had gotten her into trouble more than once.

It took them a while to find the exact apartment complex. Some of the buildings were so old and poorly maintained that the apartment numbers had long ago vanished. Negligent landlords had failed to replace them. It was just starting to mist when they finally pulled into the parking lot. Melanie grimaced before exiting the vehicle to join Jace. It wasn't that she minded the rain. She loved the rain. What she didn't love was being cold. Who knew how long it would be before she could change into dry clothes?

A snort made her look at her companion. The sardonic twist of his lips told her clearly he knew what she was thinking.

"Deal with it, Melanie. I need you to stay with me."

Melanie stuck her tongue out as she followed him. Childish. But it made her feel better.

They knocked on Alayna's door without success. Five minutes later, all levity vanished. An older woman in curlers came out to watch.

"You won't get an answer," she mentioned casually.

"Oh?" Jace gave her a professional smile. One that gave nothing away.

"Nah, haven't seen her around in a week. Super's getting steamed. She owes him rent." Her voice rang with relish.

Jace went and got the landlord to let them into the apartment. As soon as the door opened, the stench hit them like a wave. The gag reflex was immediate. Without being told, Melanie knew what they would find.

As it swung inward, she looked inside, then bolted to the stairwell, retching and gasping.

Jace found her there a few minutes later.

"Was that her?" she whimpered.

His face pale and grim, he nodded.

"How?"

He hesitated. "Stabbed. Several times. Come on. The air is fresher outside. I need to call for backup." It would be the second time that day. Quite a record for a small town in rural Pennsylvania.

Melanie was waiting for Jace forty-five minutes later when loud footsteps alerted her that someone was coming toward her. She knew it wasn't Jace. His footsteps were quieter. Brisker. Jace did everything with purpose. These footsteps sounded as though whoever was coming over was stomping. Almost as if he were angry.

She turned her head as another lieutenant approached her. Yep. He looked angry. He had a sneer on his face. Uh-oh. She could sense trouble. Where was Jace?

"So, Miss Melanie Swanson. Funny finding you at yet another crime scene." Contempt dripped from his voice.

"I had nothing to do with this."

He curled his lip and gave her the once-over, making her skin crawl.

"I just think it's odd that one of the jurors who put you behind bars is dead, and you just *happen* to be the one to find her." He narrowed his eyes at her, challenging her.

Lord Jesus, please not again, she prayed. *I don't have the strength to do this again.*

"Leave her alone, Dan." Jace approached them, focusing his ice-blue eyes on the younger lieutenant. "I'm the one who found the body, not her. And she was nowhere near here when Miss Brown was murdered."

The lieutenant reddened, flashing an angry stare at Mel.

"She could've still been involved. You know things like that happen."

Jace scoffed. "Do you really think someone who's smart enough to pull off an inside job would be dumb enough to show up at the crime scene?"

"I still say it's suspicious."

"I know you've only been with us for a couple of months, Lieutenant Willis, but you need to understand how things are done here. We don't harass civilians, no matter what they have in their past. I don't care what they would have done in Pittsburgh."

Dan's face hardened into an ugly mask. "At least in Pittsburgh we don't let known criminals tag along on investigations."

Jace narrowed his cold eyes at the belligerent man. "Have you got a problem with me, Lieutenant? Because I can send you back to the station for desk duty anytime you want."

Dan straightened.

"No, sir."

"Glad to hear it. Now, we need to process this crime scene with objectivity. If you can't handle that, I'll have the chief send me someone who can." Jace folded his arms and waited. His stance made it plain to all that he meant what he said.

Dan lowered his eyes. "Yes, sir. I mean. I can do it, sir."

"Good." Jace nodded briskly. "I want you to return to the scene and start interviewing other residents. Find out if anyone saw or heard anything. The apartment was trashed, like a robbery gone bad, but I'm not buying it."

Dan turned to follow his orders. Before he walked away, he glared at Melanie. She shivered at the sheer malevolence in his stare.

With very real fear, she knew that things had gotten a whole lot worse.

THREE

Jace pulled the cruiser into the driveway of Sarah Swanson's house and shut off the engine. The silence surrounding them was eerie. The day had started out cold and wet. Now that it was late afternoon, the wind had picked up with a definite bite. The landscape that had appeared so peaceful and charming just hours before now took on a sinister look as the sun lowered and the shadows lengthened. Tension shimmered in the air between Jace and Melanie, the day's events hanging heavy in their minds.

Jace turned to face Melanie. He frowned. Even though the light was fading, he could see that her face was pale and drawn. She had proved herself to be stronger than her fragile appearance suggested, but the rough day she'd experienced had to be taking its toll. Unbidden, the image of her using her inhaler that morning popped into his head.

"I don't like this." His fierce words shattered the silence. Melanie's eyes snapped to his, surprise in their depths.

"Don't like what?" she queried anxiously.

His eyes narrowed as he surveyed their surroundings with suspicion. He blew out a fierce breath. Though he could see nothing worrisome, his instincts told him to be careful.

"I don't like leaving you here alone. This house is completely isolated. Anything could happen and no one would know." He threw a concerned glance her way. "Come back to town with me. We'll put you up in a hotel room for the night."

She was already shaking her head. He should have known this wouldn't be easy.

"I know you mean well, but I can't go into town. All those people watching me, judging me as if they know me. I couldn't stand it, Jace." Melanie looked down at her lap. Jace couldn't be sure, but he thought there were tears in her eyes. He could hear them in her trembling voice.

"Melanie, please be sensible," he reasoned. "Someone dangerous is out to get you. One juror is dead, and your aunt came this close to sharing her fate."

A strangled sound escaped from her quivering lips. It might have been a muffled sob. Jace peered closer at her face. His chest tightened when he saw a single tear trace down her pale cheek. It shimmered in the waning light.

"I so wanted to believe that what happened to Aunt Sarah was an accident."

"You know it wasn't, though, right?"

She nodded slowly. Then stiffened. Her eyes flew to his, wide with horror.

"Jace," she gasped, "people will think I tried to kill her. You know they will. Her and that juror." She choked up. Visibly distressed, she reached out and grabbed his hand.

Jace was fairly certain she was unaware of her actions. Uncomfortable, he carefully extracted his hand from her grasp and shifted so he was farther away from her. She colored and averted her gaze, clenching her hands in her lap. He continued as if he didn't notice.

"I was with you both times," he pointed out. "I know for a fact that there was no way you could have poisoned your aunt. Wasn't I with you from almost the instant you left the prison this morning?"

She laughed bitterly, shaking her head in a confused fashion. "Was that only this morning? I feel like I've aged a year since then."

As if drawn, her eyes again moved to his. Her lips opened as if to ask a question. Then she stopped, and turned her eyes again to the house. Lifting her chin, she reached for the door handle.

"I'll be fine."

Jace sighed and unlocked the doors. They both exited the vehicle. Melanie drew her arms tightly around her waist. Jace wondered if it was the cold or fear making her shiver, but decided not to ask. He knew her well enough now to know such a question would not be met with favor. Shutting the car door, he moved beside her.

As they moved toward the house, he kept up his vigilance. If there was a danger present, he was determined to find it before he left her inside by herself. Since she refused to go to a hotel, he knew he would be spending the night in his cruiser, keeping watch.

Jace opened his mouth to try to persuade her one last time to come back to town. His pager went off before he could say anything. Calling in, he learned that he was needed for a situation downtown. The knowledge that he would have to go left him torn between relief that he could leave her disturbing presence and frustration that he would be leaving her unguarded. If only he could have requested an officer to be on guard outside her house, he would have felt better. But he knew that wouldn't happen. The events of the day had stretched the resources of their small town police department to the limit. There was literally no one else available. He momentarily considered taking her on the call with him and having her remain in the car. He quickly discounted that idea. He was going into a potentially volatile situation. She would be safer locked in the house.

Melanie put her hand on his arm. Her eyes were a little sad, but understanding.

"Go do your job. I'll be fine."

Still, he hesitated.

"Let me check out your house first," he conceded reluctantly.

A quick check of her house and grounds showed nothing suspicious. The broken window had been boarded, he was pleased to note. The uneasy knot in his stomach persisted, but Jace was sure he was being paranoid. Melanie was a grown woman. If she locked her doors and windows, and kept the phone handy, she would be fine until he returned.

"Keep your doors locked. Don't let anyone in," he ordered at the door. "As soon as this situation downtown is settled, I'll be back."

"Jace, no. You'll be exhausted," Melanie protested.

But he saw the relief in her eyes.

"I'll be back."

Jace walked out and shut the door firmly behind him. He waited until the sound of the dead bolt told him she had followed his orders. Forcing himself to move, he returned to his vehicle and turned it around. Heading back toward town, he allowed himself one last glance back in his rearview mirror. She would be fine, he told himself. He didn't need to worry about her. It was probably good for him to get some distance from her, anyway. After the day she had had, he was feeling too sympathetic toward her for his own peace of mind. He would protect her—that was his job. But he wouldn't get emotionally attached. No good could come of letting himself feel anything for her. Thanks to what had happened with Ellie, he knew that affection and duty did not mix. In his experience, affection weakened the ability to look at a situation objectively.

He dragged his mind away from his little sister.

"Lord, help me to focus on the truth," he prayed. "I think this girl could really get to me. I know I'm attracted to her. Help me to do Your will. Oh," he added, "and please protect Melanie while I am gone."

Satisfied, he pushed down on the gas pedal and answered his call to duty.

Jace finished filling out his report and sighed. Stretching, he looked at the clock and grimaced. Seven o'clock. Who would have ever thought a Monday evening could be so eventful? Man, he was bushed. And hungry. He had been so busy, he had completely skipped dinner. He decided to pick up a pizza before he headed back to Melanie's place.

A knock on the door made him look up.

"Jace, got a moment?"

Jace turned, his eyebrow raised as he watched his boss stride quickly toward him. Paul Kennedy was the kind of man who instilled trust and confidence. He did everything with purpose.

"Sure, Paul. What's up?" Jace greeted his friend more casually than he would if others were about. Even though the two men had been best friends for twenty years, they both strove to keep their working relationship professional. Neither wanted any claims of favoritism when Jace started advancing in the ranks. Good thing, too. Some of the other officers had shown jealousy early on.

"I wanted to know how things were going with the Swanson case. I heard there've been some incidents."

Nodding, Jace brought Paul up to date. Paul's face went from concerned to astonished to thoughtful.

"Jace, we've known each other most of our lives. What are you not telling me?"

Jace sighed. He should have known Paul would sense he was holding back.

"This whole situation makes me edgy. I might have bought that Sarah Swanson had an accidental allergic reaction, but her niece insists that isn't possible. Sarah was too careful."

"You trust her judgment?"

Jace shrugged. "Yeah, I do. Add to that the murder of Alayna Brown shortly after she spoke to Mrs. Swanson about being threatened, and my cop instinct is yelling at me that Miss Swanson is in danger."

"Any chance Miss Swanson is somehow behind all of this?"

Jace stood and started to pace the confines of his office as he assessed the situation, thinking out loud as he did.

"No way. Remember, I was with her from the courthouse to her aunt's house. On your orders. I saw her face when she found her aunt. There was no way she was responsible for that. And this afternoon? She didn't have anything to do with that, either. And why would she want to? She'd have nothing to gain from Alayna Brown's death, and might actually have something to lose if Miss Brown really did have information about having been threatened to give a guilty verdict." He turned to face his boss's impassive expression. "I can't help feeling she's in danger."

"We should move her to a motel for a more secure environment. Her aunt's house is surrounded by a lot of nothing. A perp could close in on her way too easily."

Jace laughed. There was no humor in the sound. "I already tried to persuade her. She won't go."

Paul sighed. Then shrugged. "Fine. Davis is back on

duty. I can have him keep watch tonight so you can have a break."

"Not necessary, Paul. I plan to park my cruiser outside her house and keep watch tonight. I know we're short staffed."

Paul raised one questioning brow. "You sure you want to do that, Jace?"

"Of course."

"Very well. You're approved to keep watch tonight. I'll schedule other officers for the next day or so. Can't let you wear yourself out." Paul started to leave, then turned back. "My brother-in-law wants to know if he can join us at the hunting camp for the first day of trout season."

Jace laughed. "I can't believe he's willing to leave the house. Isn't your sister almost ready to have her baby?"

"She still has six weeks." Paul grinned. "Allen called me last night. Seems Cammie ordered him away for the weekend. Her friends are throwing her a baby shower, and some of them are from out of town, so they'll be staying the weekend."

Jace shuddered in mock horror, then nodded. "Yeah, there's room for one more. I think I have an extra pole and enough bait if he needs it."

"He will. He's still a city boy, but we're working on him." With a wave, Paul left, whistling the theme song to *The Andy Griffith Show.*

Jace watched his boss leave his office. Frowning, he turned and moved to his desk. The sooner he could get this paperwork done, the sooner he could be on his way. He glanced at the clock again: 7:07 p.m. If he left now, he could be to the pizza place by seventy twenty, then back to Melanie's by seven forty. *I'd better call her to let her know I'm on my way,* he decided. *Wouldn't want to scare her when I drive up the lane.*

* * *

Seven ten.

Mel glanced at the clock and rubbed her arms, which were covered in goose bumps. She checked the lock and slumped against the door. Her heart was pounding so hard, she could practically hear the blood pulsing through her veins. She had been hearing noises for what seemed like hours, but in reality was only ten minutes.

Prior to that she had tried to keep busy. She had cleaned up the hot cocoa, which had been left pooled on the floor. She didn't think the stain would be permanent. She was grateful that the officers had cleaned up the broken glass from the window and boarded it before they left. She knew it wasn't their job.

There was only so much work to do, though. Her aunt had never been fond of clutter, and Mel knew for a fact that she had someone come in and clean for her several times a week. When she had done all she could, she went to her old room. She opened her closet and felt tears spring to her eyes. Aunt Sarah had told her that she had brought some of Mel's things back from the apartment she had once shared with Seth.

Once, she could have various friends to help her feel better. Not anymore. Even if she knew how to reach any of her old friends, and assuming they didn't hang up on her, what could she say? Her old crowd had abandoned her. It was probably for the best. She hadn't been a Christian when she went to jail.

She shook her head, determined to dispel these depressing thoughts. Reaching in, she grabbed one of her favorite outfits. The soft light green T-shirt and darker green shrug were roomy, but they were okay. She needed a belt to secure the jeans, though. Funny, she hadn't realized how much weight she had lost in prison. Sighing, she returned to the living room.

She tried to read one of the paperbacks her aunt had on the coffee table, but she was too aware of the passage of time. Anxiety crept up on her. It continued to increase as the shadows deepened. Several times, she caught herself reaching for the phone, to call Jace and find out when he'd return.

"Control yourself, Mel." Her voice was oddly loud in the empty house. No, she couldn't be selfish. Jace took his duty seriously. Besides, it wouldn't do to grow too dependent on him. "These noises are probably just because this is an old house."

It was the "probably" that concerned her.

She looked at the clock again and grimaced. How long would Jace be gone, anyway?

She bit her lip as she remembered that moment in the car when she had almost asked him if he still thought she was guilty. She snorted. What a dumb question.

"Don't read anything into it, Mel. Just because he took your side earlier against that officer doesn't mean he would believe you now. He is trained to focus on the evidence, not on his emotions."

Mel cast a wary glance around the room. Funny, this house had always seemed so warm and welcoming, with its warm yellow walls, the cozy fireplace and her aunt's skill with creating an inviting space. Now, however, all she could see was how the curtains didn't completely shut. Anyone could peer in. Biting her lip, she scrutinized the locks. Unlike the doors, which she knew sported state-of-the-art dead bolts, the windows all had the original locks from when the house was first built decades earlier. Weak locks. She should know. She had sneaked in and out of this house often during her teens. Her aunt had never had a clue, or Mel was sure the locks would have been replaced long ago. The idea crossed her mind to go to the kitchen to wait. She rejected that idea almost as soon as it entered her mind. She would feel even more vulnerable if she couldn't see what was happening out front.

Her eyes looked at the side window. It was boarded up tight. In her mind, though, she could still see that brick flying through it. She shuddered.

Scritch, scritch, scritch.

Yelping, she leaped up from the couch. Her heart in her throat, she frantically looked around the room. This was a new sound. Was that a mouse? Some kind of animal? Or was someone in the house with her? *Lord help me.* She sent up an urgent prayer.

A weapon. Of course. She needed some kind of weapon. But what? Her aunt had never kept guns in the house. Her eyes alighted on the fireplace tools.

Scritch, scritch.

She whimpered. Terrified, she slowly crept across the room as soundlessly as she could. She grabbed the first tool she touched. It had a nasty-looking hook on the end. Grimacing, she moved in the direction of the sound. When it came again, she realized it was coming from the large picture window in the front room. Letting out an explosive breath, she moved to adjust the blinds. Really, she was such a coward. Terrified by what was probably a tree branch against the window. Scoffing at herself, she peered out into the now-dark yard. Her breath caught. Terror returned. A man was running down her driveway toward the trees.

"No. This can't be happening."

When the phone rang, she shrieked. *Oh, maybe it's Jace. Maybe he's calling to check up on me.* She swiped up the phone as if it were a lifeline.

"Hello?"

"Not so brave now, are ya, little girl?" an unfamiliar male voice jeered.

"Who are you?"

"You disappoint me. Such a common question." He chuckled. It was not a pleasant sound. "I don't think that poker would have worked against a gun, though. Do you?"

With a sharp cry, she dropped the phone back into the cradle. He had been watching her! The man she had seen, he had spied on her. Suddenly she knew it hadn't been branches she had heard. That man had deliberately tried to spook her. He wanted her to know he could get to her whenever he felt like it.

The phone rang again. Mel let it go to the answering machine, covering her ears as the voice filled the room.

Shaking her head, Mel backed fearfully away from it. He could call all night. That didn't mean she had to answer. She couldn't force herself to leave the room, though. Settling herself against the wall with the poker in her hands, she waited. Watched. Maybe she wasn't a match for him if he came for her. That didn't mean she had to give up. Steel entered her soul. No one was going to scare her off. Not without a fight.

The phone rang again. Mel trembled as the answering machine kicked on. She waited for the voice to begin taunting her.

"Hi, Melanie. It's me, Jace. I am…" She flew to the phone.

"Jace!" Melanie's voice was choked with tears as she grabbed the phone with sweaty hands.

"Melanie! Are you okay?"

"I'm okay, but…" The rest of her words were garbled by sobs.

"Melanie, hold on. I'll be there in twenty minutes."

Melanie heard the siren blare before he cut the connection. She dropped the old-fashioned phone back into its cradle. Immediately it rang again. She huddled back against the wall as the answering machine kicked on. She covered her ears with her hands to shut out the string of threats and insults.

Red-and-blue police lights flashed. Cautiously, she crawled to the picture window and peered out. Her eyes widened. Jace had made it in fifteen minutes. She watched as he left his car and practically ran up her steps.

She flew to the door and threw it open before he could knock. The temptation to throw herself into his strong arms was overwhelming, but she managed to resist the urge. Even scared out of her mind, she knew she would regret acting on the impulse. Grabbing his hand, she pulled him forcefully into the house, shutting the door and slamming the dead bolt behind him.

"I'm being watched," she whispered, answering his question before he asked it.

His face hardened. "Explain."

"Shortly after seven, I heard noises at the window. I thought a tree branch was scraping the glass." She swallowed, her trembling hand going to her throat. "But when I went to look, there was a man, running down the drive…"

Spinning on his heel, Jace raced to the window. He peered outside for a few seconds before grabbing his gun and a flashlight from his pocket. Melanie clutched at his arm as he stalked to the door. The determined look on his face told her exactly what he planned to do. He shook her off gently. Ignoring her protests, he unbolted the door and moved outside, eyes peeled.

Mel waited inside, her heart pounding. She couldn't bear the thought of something bad happening to Jace. Oh, what was taking him so long? Surely he should be back by now. Picking up her coat, Mel decided to go check on him. He walked back inside as she was zipping the coat. Bolting the door, he turned. Stopped. Suddenly he grinned.

"You weren't by any chance thinking of coming after me, were you?"

A fierce flush spread over her cheeks. Defiantly, she tossed her head.

"I just thought you might need some help." Melanie hated the defensiveness in her voice.

Jace shook his head. The amusement drained from his face. The sudden seriousness of his expression made her shiver. Whatever he had seen out there, it hadn't been good.

"There were footsteps under your window and leading down the driveway. And I found this." He held out a round black object, roughly two inches in diameter. Mel leaned forward for a closer look, inhaling his aftershave as she did.

"Is that what I think it is? It looks like a lens cover. Did that man have a camera with him?" Melanie fought down a wave of panic. Now was the time for clear thinking, not hysterics.

"Sure is, and not just any camera, either. Whoever was using this meant business."

The phone rang. The relative calm Jace's return had brought was shattered as she paled. Jace walked to stand before her, his concerned gaze sweeping her face. Instinctively, she clutched at his jacket and buried her face in it. She tried not to listen as the answering machine kicked on and the malicious voice filled the room.

"Don't think that cop'll protect you, little girl. Sooner or later, you'll be alone again, and when you are—"

The voice was abruptly cut off as Jace picked up the phone. He listened to the invective spewing from the voice for an instant. Then he hung up, none too gently.

Melanie became aware of the exhausted tears pouring

down her face. She allowed Jace to lead her over to the couch. He pushed her down onto the corner cushion, then reached for the afghan lying across the back. Wrapping it around her shoulders, he knelt before her.

"When did these phone calls start?"

"Right after I saw the man outside. He started talking about what I had been doing, so I knew he had been watching me." She shivered and pulled the afghan tighter. "He's been calling every couple of minutes. I've lost track of how many phone calls."

She leaned her head back and closed her eyes. She was so tired.

"Why didn't you unplug your phone?"

"I was afraid he'd see me if I walked to the phone," she admitted. "I've been crouched on the floor, out of sight."

He closed his eyes and shook his head. "If I had been here…"

"It's not your fault. You're here now, and he's still calling."

The phone rang again. Melanie shuddered. Jace grabbed his cell phone.

"I'm going to call my boss about putting a trace on your line. Maybe this guy will slip up."

He shut his phone slowly when the voice filled the room.

"If I were you, I'd be careful going out the back door. Never know what you might find." Malicious laughter echoed before it was abruptly cut off.

Mel watched in horror as Jace reached into his holster and retrieved his gun. He moved with care toward the back door, hugging the walls and staying away from the windows. The idiot was going to open the back door. It had to be a trap.

"Wait! Jace! You can't go out there! Are you crazy?"

He blew out his breath, hard, and tossed her a mocking

smile. "What? You think I should wait for the police? Oh, that's right. I *am* the police."

She held her breath and whispered a prayer as he stood with his back against the wall next to the door, his gun held ready.

"Keep back," he ordered in a low voice.

Then slowly, he reached out and closed his hand around the knob and started turning.

FOUR

Her heart in her throat, Mel kept her eyes glued on Jace as he turned the knob. The door opened with agonizing slowness. Any moment she'd hear some spooky music like in a horror movie. She shook her head as the errant thought flitted across her weary brain. A familiar tightness in her chest warned her that she would soon be in need of her inhaler again. But there was no way she was going to reach for it now. Any movement might distract Jace.

Jace opened the door and peered out. He let out a rough sound of disgust, almost a growl. He pulled the door open wider and stepped outside. As he disappeared from her sight, panic screamed in the pit of her belly, fighting to crawl its way out. She hung on to her control, but it was a struggle. When he returned, she let out a breath, unaware until she did so that she had been holding it.

Jace tucked his gun back into his holster with a single abrupt movement. With his other hand, he whipped out his cell phone and hit a button. A scowl furrowed his brow and curled his lips. He stalked back to the door and peered out. Curious, Mel leaned over to peer past him. And gasped in shock.

A storefront mannequin swung in the breeze, a make-shift noose around its plastic neck. A brunette wig was balanced precariously upon its head in an obvious attempt to make it resemble Melanie. A sign had been hung around its neck. It read Murderer. You Are Not Wanted Here. Mesmerized, she was only vaguely aware that Jace was conferring with someone on his phone. He disconnected after a minute. She stayed focused on the Melanie mannequin. Freaked out. Wait. Was that…? She looked closer…

"Oh!"

Jace swung around at her cry.

"Melanie, it's not real, it's just a mannequin," he held up his hands in a calming motion.

"It's a mannequin wearing my clothes!" Her throat was so tight, it hurt to force the words past the constriction. "I wore that dress all the time. It was a favorite of mine when I was still in high school."

"Are you sure? Maybe it's a coincidence—just a similar dress."

Melanie shook her head. There was no way she was mistaken.

"I know that dress," she insisted. "Aunt Sarah made it. If you look at the tag, you'll see its one of her personalized tags."

She had always felt so pretty, so feminine in the delicate blue dress. It was the only modest dress she had owned back then. It had pleased her aunt no end when Mel wore it.

Someone had ruined a precious memory. But how had he even gotten the dress?

"I don't know, Melanie." Mel's eyes shot wide. Had she asked that out loud? Apparently she had.

She was even more surprised when Jace patted her shoulder. The gesture was a little awkward, but she was touched by his attempt at compassion.

Jace cleared his throat. "Don't worry. We'll figure it out."

An hour later, she listened silently to Jace and his superior, who had arrived twenty minutes earlier. Her eyes followed Jace as he paced back and forth across the length of the living room. His eyes were hooded. His mouth was tightened into a grim line. He kept removing his hat and raking his hand across his hair in what seemed to be a habitual gesture when he was agitated. She could vaguely recall him making the same gesture four years ago.

"Something's off."

Melanie jumped. Jace stomped to a halt before her and glared at the people watching him.

"Well, don't blame me," Chief Kennedy drawled. "I'm one of the good guys."

"Ha ha." Jace resumed pacing. "I mean whoever this dude is, he's not acting right."

"What part of bad guy do you need me to explain, Lieutenant?"

Despite the seriousness of the situation, Melanie found herself muffling a giggle at the Chief's wry remark. Unfortunately, Jace apparently had really good hearing. He leveled a flat stare her way. She straightened in her chair, then gave him a serious nod, biting her lip to keep herself from laughing again.

"You know what I mean. He's a perp. Means he should have a pattern. But this guy is breaking pattern. Melanie should be dead."

The room swayed. Mel felt the blood draining from her face. Hearing her fate stated with such devastating coolness shook her to her soul. Mouth dry, she stared at Jace.

He flashed a look her way. Was that sympathy? Pity?

"Sorry, Melanie. Shouldn't have been so blunt."

Chief Kennedy scratched his chin thoughtfully. "Go on. I'd like to hear more."

Jace hunkered down on the footstool in front of Mel, settling his elbows on his knees and leaning toward her. "Alayna Brown was murdered after going to see your aunt—though there was an attempt to make it look like a simple burglary gone wrong. Your aunt was poisoned. I have to assume it was meant to look like an accident. If we had arrived later..."

"My release time was changed!" Mel burst out, interrupting him. She shot out of her chair and walked around the perimeter of the room. She rubbed her hands up and down her arms to ward off a chill. "I wasn't supposed to be released until noon, but it was moved up. But how did the person who poisoned her not know that? Everyone knew. At least it felt that way this morning."

"But your release time was changed less than twelve hours before it happened," Chief Kennedy pointed out. "They may not have known that. Or they might not have been able to change the timing on the poisoning. Sneaking the tainted food into your aunt's kitchen might have been something that could only be done at a certain time."

"Whatever the reason for the timing with Mrs. Swanson," Jace broke in, "they are playing with us now."

Mel stopped pacing.

Chief Kennedy sat forward, eyes intent.

"This guy didn't actually try to kill Melanie. He's trying to scare her. He's playing." A stark note entered his voice at this pronouncement.

A thick silence filled the room. Mel patted her inhaler to reassure herself.

Then Chief Kennedy spoke, his voice now full of authority, all hint of joking gone.

"He doesn't want Miss Swanson dead, he just wants her gone. But why?"

* * *

Jace and Chief Kennedy talked strategy and compared theories for another twenty minutes. Mel felt as if her head were stuffed with wool. The energy seeped from her system as she listened to their clinical conversation. They could have been discussing the latest football game, they were so casual. Only the occasional concerned looks Jace shifted in her direction kept her from screaming in frustration at their callousness. His glances assured her that he wasn't feeling as nonchalant as he sounded. Or at least she hoped he wasn't. It was too much.

Bone-weary, she allowed her eyelids to flutter shut.

Within moments she was sound asleep. She awoke to find Jace leaning over her, shaking her shoulder. "Melanie, I have to go out to the car."

"What?" She sat up confused. How long had she been asleep?

"My car, sleepyhead," Jace replied, looking amused. "I can't stay in here overnight. And there is no way I am leaving you here alone."

"Chief Kennedy? Is he—"

"Paul left five minutes ago. He knows I'm staying."

"I really want to be independent and tell you to go home, that I'll be fine and all that nonsense." Mel looked him straight in the eye. "I can't, though."

Unexpectedly, Jace reached out and brushed a hand lightly over her hair. "You gonna be all right in here?"

She nodded. The top of her head tingled where his hand had stroked. She could feel her cheeks and ears growing warm.

"Yeah," she managed to choke out, "I'll be okay. Thanks."

"No problem. Just make sure you make plenty of strong coffee in the morning, and we'll be fine." Jace winked, then went to his car. Mel watched him go, then shut up the house. She remembered the dress on the mannequin and shuddered. Someone had to have been in her bedroom. There was no way she could sleep in her old room knowing that. She could have slept in the spare room, but she was reluctant to go farther back in the house. Piling up a couple of small pillows, she lay back down on the couch. She was closer to Jace here. He would protect her if anyone tried to get to her. In her mind, she could hear a voice threatening her. Her mind relived the terror-filled moments before Jace arrived until she fell into an exhausted slumber.

In the cruiser, Jace was wide-awake. Absently, he gnawed on a piece of cold pizza as he went over the events in his mind. He had never seen anyone as frightened as Melanie had been when she answered the door. He could literally see her fighting not to throw herself into his arms. For a woman as proud as she was, that was saying something. He was also uncomfortably aware of how disappointed he had felt when she withdrew. So much for keeping his distance.

Leaning his head back against the headrest, he closed his eyes and tried to recall the voice of Melanie's mysterious caller. It had been obviously disguised. But still, there was something about it that was familiar. If only he could remember why. Something in the accent. It wouldn't come to him. Frustrated, he pounded his fist on the steering wheel. His hand slipped and accidentally bumped the horn. The single honk was embarrassingly loud. Jerking the offending hand back, he stuffed it in his pocket. Couldn't cause him any trouble there. Sighing, his mind returned to the voice.

He knew that voice.

But from where?

He drifted off into a fitful sleep. Several times during

the night, he awakened abruptly. At around three in the morning, he decided to take a look around the perimeter of the house. He unfolded his lanky frame from the car, stretching and yawning, and then wincing as his muscles protested. He pulled a face and rubbed the small of his back. Sleeping in a car was never a pleasant experience. He felt almost as tired as if he hadn't slept at all. Not to mention the tightness that was still knotting his shoulders. He was going to have a monster of a tension headache if he didn't take measures soon.

Digging in the glove compartment, he found two pain pills in the first-aid kit and chased them down with yesterday's cold coffee. Yech. But the only other option was to swallow them dry. Nothing worse than pill paste on your tongue.

He started around the house at an easy stride. One hand held the flashlight, the other his service weapon. He swept a wide beam across the yard. To his relief, he could see nothing out of place. Sidling up to the window, a frown pulled the corners of his mouth down. The curtains were drawn, but a small sliver was still open at the outside edge. He peered inside. He could barely make out Melanie's shape under a pile of blankets on the couch. Her face was turned away from the window, but a mop of brown hair was visible.

He couldn't do anything about that now. He'd make sure to mention it to her in the morning. He completed his circle around the house and returned to the cruiser. When he drifted off to sleep again, his rest was easier.

Three hours later, he jolted awake again. A feeling of unease slithered down his spine. Something was wrong. He could sense it. Gathering up his gun and his phone, he threw open the door and loped across the lawn to Melanie's front door. The entire way he muttered a litany of prayer under his breath. He might not know where the danger lay, but God knew.

"Lord, You are in control. Help us."

When he arrived at the door, his blood froze.

Attached to the door with black electrical tape were three pictures. Him, asleep in his cruiser. Melanie, out like a light on the couch. Except in this picture, her face was visible.

The third picture showed Jace and Melanie together as they stared at the mannequin the night before. His muscles bunched and a spasm of rage shot through his gut as he remembered Melanie's terror. Someone was playing a game, all right. Jace didn't intend to let them win.

He ran back to the car and grabbed a pair of rubber gloves and a sealable bag from the glove box. Pulling out his cell phone, he took several pictures of the doorway for evidence and sent them in an attachment to Paul. Then, working quickly, he used his pocketknife to scrape the tape holding the pictures off the door. Pulling the pictures free, he placed them in the bag, sealed it and then slipped it into his coat pocket.

He realized he could procrastinate no longer. The unmistakable sounds of someone moving about inside told him Mel was awake. Reluctantly, he raised his fist and rapped on the door.

FIVE

Melanie opened her eyes to see the sun shining in on the floor. She bounded from the couch to the window. Peering outside, she felt relief bubble inside. Everything looked normal. Nothing appeared disturbed, and she could see the cruiser parked in the driveway. It was easier to be brave in the daylight. She squinted her eyes. Huh. The car was empty. Where was Jace? A firm knock answered that question. Momentarily forgetting caution, she ran to the front door and threw it open. Only to be met by his fierce scowl.

"What?" she demanded, feeling defensive.

"Did you even check to make sure it was me?"

"Well, of course it was you!"

"No 'of course' about it." Jace stepped into the room. Feeling crowded, Mel retreated a step. He followed her. He bent, bringing his face closer to hers. "From now on, you check. I don't care who you think is on the other side. Check. Clear?"

Mel nodded, resisting the urge to salute. Now would have been a good time to have a witty answer. Nothing came to mind, though.

She cleared her throat.

"I was getting ready to fix breakfast. Are you hungry?"

His stomach gurgled loudly before he could answer.

The tension broke and he grinned. Her breath caught in her throat. When he smiled like that, he seemed to shed the hard shell.

"I don't think I need to answer," he joked. She rolled her eyes. "I'm feeling rather rank. I should clean up first. Okay if I grab my bag and take a shower first?"

"No, go right ahead. The bathroom's upstairs, first door on the right."

"Right. I'll be back." He returned a minute later, an army duffel bag slung over his shoulder. He shut the door and latched the dead bolt. "If you hear or see anything, you come and get me. I'm serious. I wouldn't even leave to shower, but the chief would expect me to respect the uniform."

She breathed a sigh of relief after he left. She felt really stupid for forgetting to check who was outside. Mistakes like that could be disastrous.

Realizing she was still in the clothes she had fallen asleep in, Melanie ran to her bedroom. Her shoulders tensed as she stood in her doorway. *Don't be ridiculous, Mel. No one is here but Jace.* Forcing herself to move, she threw on some clothes. As she was running a brush through her hair, she allowed her mind to wander over the events of the past twenty-four hours. Who could possibly hate her that much?

She shook herself out of her reverie. Breakfast. She had a hungry man to feed. She meandered into the kitchen and poked around the refrigerator to see if Aunt Sarah had anything around for breakfast. "Aha!" she cried as she pulled out the ingredients to make a hash brown casserole. Within minutes, it was in the oven baking.

While it baked, she settled down at the kitchen table for her morning devotions. Knowing they would be interrupted at any minute, she tried to make the most of the time she had. Grabbing her Bible and her journal, she sat at the table with one leg hooked beneath the other. She alternated between reading the Bible before her and writing.

The prison chaplain who had led her to the Lord had encouraged her to keep a prayer journal. It had become part of her daily routine over the past three years. She had found that journaling while praying helped her organize her thoughts. Plus, she had often found that if she read back over previous entries, she could see the hand of God at work. It was a technique she had seen Aunt Sarah use throughout her teen years. She hadn't appreciated those silent lessons then, but she was thankful for them now.

A voice floated down the stairs to her. Jace apparently liked to sing in the shower. She snickered, then slapped a hand over her mouth as giggles continued to erupt. He sounded like a wounded frog. Who would have thought that the competent Lieutenant Tucker, so skilled and confident in so many other ways, couldn't carry a tune in a bucket? It was endearing. He tried for a high note. Missed. It was a good thing he didn't sing in the car.

The water shut off. Thankfully, so did the singing. Ten minutes later, Jace appeared in the kitchen. He stopped next to the table, closed his eyes, and inhaled deeply.

"Breakfast is almost…"

Jace held up a hand to halt her speech, his eyes still closed.

"Please, I'm busy." He inhaled again. "Man, something smells good."

"Can I speak now?"

He opened one eye. "Okay."

She opened her mouth to speak, then closed it when she realized she had no idea what she wanted to say. The intimacy of the situation made her feel awkward. Although she trusted Jace to keep her safe, he was not someone she wanted herself to grow attracted to. It was kinda hard to forget that he had been the person to send her to jail. But even though she knew he still believed in her guilt, he had truly gone out of his way to keep her safe for the past day.

When he opened his other eye and their eyes met, her breath caught. She used to scoff whenever books said silly things like "electricity zinged between them." Now she understood what that meant.

The buzzer on the oven broke the mood. Laughing nervously, she stood up to get the casserole out. Jace walked over and filled the two coffee mugs sitting on the counter.

"Cream's in the fridge. Sugar's there…on the counter." She jerked her chin in the general direction.

Soon they were eating breakfast. The moment he forked a tasty bite into his mouth, Jace groaned. "This is fantastic."

"Better than your mom makes?" she teased.

Jace looked around as if making sure they were alone. "Don't you dare repeat this," he confided, "but my mom can't make toast."

Mel choked on her food as a laugh caught her by surprise.

"You're making that up!" she accused.

"Scout's honor." He held up two fingers in a mock Scout salute.

"Hmm. Were you ever a Scout?"

"No. But it's still true. My dad was the cook in the family. When he died, my two sisters and I decided we had to learn to cook to survive."

Melanie's expression was sympathetic. "How old were you?"

"I was fifteen. The oldest."

"And your sisters?"

In a flash, the mood changed. The open expression on

his face changed, became distant. He broke eye contact with her and focused intently on his food.

"Jace?"

He shrugged, still not meeting her eyes.

Mel watched in astonishment as the playful man eating with her disappeared, leaving a cold, silent stranger. What on earth had happened? Clearly, his family was an off-limits topic. He'd brought them up, though, not her.

Maybe it was just as well that he'd turned cold. She needed the reminder that they weren't friends—that she shouldn't trust him. She knew some men could turn on you without warning. Especially charming men, like her father. And Seth. Hadn't she learned her lesson? Setting her mouth in a mutinous line, she finished her meal quickly, then stood and started clearing the table. When he rose to assist her, she raised an imperious hand to stall him.

"I am able to clear the table myself, Lieutenant Tucker. Perhaps you have some phone calls to make." Although her words were polite, her tone was cold enough to freeze the coffee in their mugs. She forced her shoulders back in a rigid stance. It hurt that he had shut her out so completely, but she would not give him the satisfaction of knowing how much.

His stupefied expression was almost comical. He took a step toward her, his hand raised as if he might touch her.

She stepped back.

"Fine," he snapped. "I need to call my chief, anyway."

Jace stalked out of the kitchen. In the living room, he pulled out his phone and tried to call Paul. When he got his voice mail, he left a brief message. As he hit End, his eyes moved to the kitchen door. His stomach turned as he remembered his abrupt conversation with Melanie. Well, he had handled that well. Disgust welled up within him. Not disgust with Melanie. With himself. He had hurt her. He knew he had, even though she had retreated back behind her protective shell. He didn't blame her. But he wasn't ready to explain himself.

How could he tell her about Ellie? Or the agony his family had suffered? That information was too personal. He had to remember that regardless of what the current situation was, Melanie Swanson was a convict—a killer. It would be wrong to share Ellie with her. Just thinking of his sweet baby sister made his chest hurt. He started to rub his chest, then shoved his fist into his pocket when he realized what he was doing.

His hand brushed against the pictures. Unbelievable. He had actually forgotten about them. Now was as good a time as any to show them to Melanie. His determined steps echoed on the hardwood. The minute he stopped in the kitchen door, guilt crept upon him. She had been crying. There were no tears now, but her eyes were red and slightly puffy. What kind of guy was he? Making her cry after yesterday's events.

Seriously not cool.

Unfortunately, he had no clue how to deal with tears.

So he didn't. Instead, he plunked himself down at the table with a single word, said in a decidedly grumpy voice.

"Sorry."

Smooth. Yep. That was him.

Melanie stared at him for long moment. Then nodded and joined him at the table.

"I meant to tell you about these first thing, but I got distracted." Jace pulled the pictures out of his pocket and laid them on the table. Through the plastic bag, they could see the picture of them embracing. It was slightly blurry due to the bag, but there was no doubt who was in the picture.

"Where…where did you get these?" Melanie asked in a trembling voice.

He winced. He wished he could shield her, but knew any sort of sugarcoating would only make a bad situation worse.

"They were taped to your door. I saw them when I woke up. They weren't there at three." He took a deep breath, then told her the rest. "The last picture is of you. Sleeping. Your curtains don't close the whole way."

The coffee mug she had been holding between her hands slipped, shattering on the floor. He could see that hot coffee splashed her jeans, but she ignored it. Her face was so pale, he was afraid she would faint. Leaping to his feet, Jace hurried to her side and knelt on one knee beside her. He placed one arm on the back of her chair to steady her, his hand touching her shoulder. With the other, he gripped her hands on her lap. Man, they were cold. And so small. He had never noticed what tiny hands she had before. He pushed the irrelevant thought from his mind.

"Melanie? Say something. Come on. Talk to me."

"He was watching me sleep?" she finally whispered.

"I know." He rubbed circles on her hand with his thumb. "Look, I called Paul while I was upstairs. It's all arranged. At some point today, I'll be relieved. I'll go home and take a nap. That way tonight I can stay awake during my shift. Another officer will relieve me at five." He nudged her, trying to urge a smile. "Unless I can convince you to let me place you in a motel in town?"

He sighed when she stubbornly shook her head. "Didn't think so."

The phone rang. Melanie shrieked, her eyes flying wide open.

Jace's face became cold as he marched to the phone and yanked it off its cradle. "Lieutenant Tucker," he barked.

He listened for a moment. He closed his eyes and raked his hands through his hair. This was not good.

Dread curdled in the pit of his stomach.

"Thank you. Yes, yes. I will let her know. We'll be there."

He turned around, then stepped back. Melanie was standing close enough to kiss. *Where did that thought come from?* Especially given the hollow look on her face.

"What will you tell me?" she demanded. "And where are we going?"

"That was the hospital. I'm sorry. Your aunt is in a coma."

For a brief moment, Jace worried that she would pass out. She swayed briefly, but managed to regain her composure. He had automatically reached out to steady her, but she pushed his hands away.

"I'm fine," she snapped, jerking away from him. She took a step toward the kitchen door and wobbled. He reached out to steady her again, but she waved him off. "I need to see my aunt."

He could see it was no use arguing with her. "Let's go."

Melanie raced into the hospital, desperate to see her aunt. The nurses directed her to the intensive care unit. She arrived at her aunt's door breathless. Two policemen stood at the entrance to her aunt's private room. When she made to enter, they blocked her.

"I'm here to see my aunt. Let me through," she demanded.

"Sorry, ma'am. We were directed to keep all unauthorized personnel out," the policeman on the right informed her. His partner merely nodded.

Melanie stomped her foot, then stopped, appalled. She

was not going to throw a tantrum. Even if she did feel like a kettle about to start whistling.

"We are authorized," Jace said smoothly from behind her.

Melanie groaned. She had completely forgotten him. Had he seen her childish behavior? She flicked a sheepish glance in his direction. Yep. His eyes were definitely twinkling with amusement as he winked at her. She lifted her chin. She had every reason to be impatient. These idiots were blocking her path.

They are protecting Aunt Sarah.

Ashamed of her uncharitable attitude, she apologized to the men. They blinked. Apparently they didn't expect good manners from an ex-con, Mel thought, torn between amusement and sadness.

"Can we enter, gentlemen?" Jace drawled politely.

"Yes, sir, Lieutenant Tucker." They moved aside to allow Mel and Jace to enter.

"Oh, Jace," Mel gasped in shock. Aunt Sarah was even more fragile in appearance than before. Tubes seemed to be fastened everywhere. A monitor set up behind her head beeped at consistent intervals. Instead of the brightly lit hospital room from yesterday, this room was kept dimmer. Melanie shivered at the macabre feeling in the air.

The door opened, admitting a young physician. The first thought that crossed Melanie's mind was that he appeared too cold to be a doctor. She immediately shoved the thought away. Who was she to judge whether the man was qualified to be a doctor? Still, his level stare made her shiver.

"Where is Dr. Jensen?" Melanie demanded.

"Dr. Jensen is out today. I am Dr. Ramirez." He smiled, a clinical smile without warmth. She was suddenly reminded of the way her father smiled. Charming on the outside, pure venom within.

Jace shook the doctor's hand. Mel thrust aside her dislike and listened as he explained her aunt's condition. Or tried to listen. It all sounded like gibberish to Melanie. She had reached the point where she could not process what he telling her.

Jace threw her a concerned glance.

"Melanie?"

"I'm sorry. I just don't get it. Yesterday I was told she would be able to come home today."

The doctor cleared his throat. "Yes, that was correct. But there an accident. The charts were switched around. Your aunt was given the wrong IV."

"The wrong IV? How does that happen?" Melanie couldn't believe what she was hearing.

"We are investigating the matter, Miss Swanson. Rest assured that we will get this sorted out."

"What was she given?"

"She was given medication to lower her glucose levels. It sent her levels too low, and caused her to go into a diabetic coma."

Snorting, she glared at the doctor. "Can you tell me for certain that my aunt will recover?"

Silence. The doctor met her eyes with his. Again, she shivered at the emptiness there. As if her aunt were just a chart instead of a living, breathing human being in need.

"Who had access to the charts?" Jace snapped.

"What? Well, I don't know…"

"Find out. And keep this information as private as possible. This is now a crime scene."

At these words, the doctor's mouth tightened. Melanie clenched and unclenched her fists in an effort to regain control of her emotions. The fact that Jace felt her aunt had been deliberately targeted came as no surprise. Indeed, she had suspected foul play the minute Jace had told her about the coma. It had to have been the same person who had tampered with her hot chocolate before. They needed to talk with the other jurors and find out what was going on—why the people connected to her and to her trial were being targeted.

"I need to locate the other eleven jurors," Jace stated, echoing her thoughts.

"Can I..." she began.

He was already shaking his head. "No. One is already dead. I can't expose you to that kind of danger."

She sighed. She hadn't really expected him to take her along, but she dreaded being apart from him. Only when he was near did she feel safe. It was strange, since he had once been her biggest enemy. But she knew in her soul that he would do anything to protect her, no matter how he felt about her personally.

Two hours later, when she left the hospital, she had even more cause to regret his absence. The Lieutenant assigned to guard her was none other than Dan Willis. She remembered his sneering remarks outside Alayna Brown's apartment. The look of disgust he gave her before leading her to his cruiser chilled her to the bone. He almost vibrated with anger and resentment as he drove her home.

She stared out the window silently. *It will be over soon*, she told herself. Another ten minutes and she would be home. She could lock herself in her house until Jace relieved Lieutenant Willis. She just had to hold on until then.

Intense relief filled her as they pulled into the driveway. As soon as the car rolled to a stop, her hand was on the door handle, ready to open it. Locked. Of course. He had to unlock it. The seconds crawled by. He didn't unlock her door. She turned to face him.

"Please unlock my door." She kept her voice steady with supreme effort.

He leisurely reached back and hit the button with a smirk. As soon as she heard the *click*, she turned and opened her door. He let her leave the vehicle without a word, but she imagined that she could feel his cold stare as she ran up the steps and unlocked the front door. Her hands shook so much that it took her three tries before she managed to get it open. She knew Lieutenant Willis was watching her when his harsh laughter reached her ears.

Blindly, she bolted the doors and closed the blinds as tightly as possible. Two minutes later, disbelief made her open the door again. He was leaving! Shocked, she watched as Lieutenant Willis sketched her a mocking wave, then drove away. Dazed, she closed the door again. Her stomach was so queasy, she thought she might vomit.

Running into the bathroom, she bent over the sink and splashed cold water on her face. Reaching back for a towel, she dried off.

A movement to her left startled her. She screamed as the bathroom door was slammed shut. She could hear something thudding against the door. Rushing to the door, she tried to open it. It was stuck! Whoever had slammed it must have put something against it. It wouldn't budge. Backing up, she slid down the wall and covered her face with her hands. Certain she was going to die, she prayed for strength and courage.

SIX

Jace frowned as he shut his car door, looking at the otherwise empty driveway. Dan had been instructed to wait until he was relieved. Maybe Sarah had taken a turn for the worse and he had driven Melanie back to the hospital? A quick call to the hospital eliminated that possibility. Sarah's status had not changed, nor had her niece come back. Jace slowly climbed the steps. His blood froze. The front door was open two inches. He knew how meticulously Melanie locked her doors. He raced inside, shouting her name.

As soon as he entered the house, he smelled it. Smoke. He could see tendrils of black smoke creeping and curling their way out of the kitchen. Without pausing, he used the radio on his shoulder to alert the EMS operator to dispatch the appropriate fire department and the paramedics. He cautiously peered into the kitchen. The stove was engulfed in flames, but Melanie was nowhere in sight. Grabbing the fire extinguisher off the wall, he yanked out the pin and doused the fire. Outside, the siren at the local volunteer fire department rent the air. Fortunately, the blaze hadn't gotten too out of control. Had he been another two or three minutes—he shuddered. He looked at the mess on the stove and frowned. A pot of water was on the burner. A small aluminum can was tipped over, oozing grease. He knew many older people kept their grease to reuse. Horrible practice.

Where was Melanie?

Knowing it could take up to fifteen minutes for help to arrive, he started to hunt for Melanie. Room by room, he searched the house. When he ran into Melanie's bedroom, he found her bathroom barricaded by a two-by-four jammed between the door and the desk.

"Melanie!" No answer. He shoved the heavy wooden piece out of the way and opened the door. Inside, Melanie was curled up in a fetal position next to the bathtub. Her eyes were open, but she was icy to the touch. Her breath wheezed in and out. Her jeans pockets were empty. Where was her inhaler? He ran back to the bedroom. Her purse was sitting on the dresser. Ignoring everything his mother had taught him about a lady's purse being private, he foraged inside until he found her medication.

"Come on, Melanie," he urged, holding the inhaler to her lips. "Inhale." He pressed the canister down as she gasped and inhaled. A minute later, he repeated the procedure, noting with relief that the wheezing had passed.

"Okay, Melanie, let's get you outta here." He picked her up and carried her out of the bathroom. She laid her head on his shoulder.

One thing was clear. This was no accident—though it was certainly set up to *look* like one. Whoever had started the fire had obviously figured the wooden beam blocking the bathroom door would be burned up in the fire. Fury boiled in the pit of his stomach. His body shook from the force of his anger. The only thing that kept him from giving in to his anger was Melanie. Feeling her shivering in his arms, he clamped down on the urge to bolt out the door and hunt down the monster who had committed this heinous act. Instead, he tightened his grip on her.

A defeated sigh caught his attention. Melanie's head was still against his shoulder. He shifted her weight so he could look at her face. An ache filled him as he saw that she was staring blankly ahead, her normally bright eyes dull.

He set her on her feet briefly at the foot of the bed. He grabbed the warm quilt covering it and wrapped it around her slender form, then hefted her gently into his arms again. His footsteps echoed in the hallway as he carried his burden to the living room and placed her carefully on the couch. He opened the windows to allow the smell of smoke to dissipate.

When the fire department arrived, he left her briefly to direct them to the kitchen. He pulled the chief aside. "This is a crime scene. You need to treat this like an arson attempt."

He returned to Melanie and found her in the same position as when he'd left her. Other than that sigh, she had not uttered a sound since he found her. He touched her face. Her skin was clammy. A new fear blossomed. Shock. He knew the symptoms well. What he needed to do now was keep her warm.

"Okay, Melanie," he said softly, keeping his voice calm. "Let's just lie you down here. I need to put some pillows under your feet, get your legs raised." He reached out and snagged the throw pillows off the back of the couch and expertly placed them so that her legs were raised. He kept up a flow of reassuring conversation. "The paramedics are on the way. We need to keep you warm until they arrive."

Melanie made no response. Jace located another blanket and covered her with it. Within moments, Jace had a roaring blaze in the fireplace. The flames cast a cozy glow about the room, but Jace was too focused on Melanie to pay any attention. He paced back and forth in front of the couch, stopping every now and then to check her pulse and make sure she was warming up. He noted with relief that her color was returning.

Ten minutes later, a loud knock shattered the stillness like a gunshot. Melanie cried out in fear. Jace rushed over and knelt beside her.

"Shhh. I called the paramedics and the police. I won't let anything hurt you. You have my word on that, Melanie." He stared into her eyes until she appeared to relax. When she settled back against the cushions, he stood and crossed the room. He opened the door to find the chief and Dan Willis standing on the porch. While he was relieved that his chief had arrived, the presence of the second made him scowl. He couldn't help but feel that Lieutenant Willis's dereliction of duty was part of the cause of Melanie's current situation. After all, had he remained at his post as ordered, the perp would not have been able to enter the building and carry out his vicious attack. Jace shuddered to think what might have happened. He carefully wiped all emotion from his face.

"Chief. Willis."

"Jace." Chief Kennedy returned his greeting with brows raised. "How is Miss Swanson? Your call seemed quite urgent."

Dan snorted. Jace swung a fierce glare in his direction.

"You have something to say, Lieutenant?" Jace ground out the title. It burned him that a lawman could behave so irresponsibly.

Dan lifted his chin, defiance glinting in his eyes.

"Nope."

Jace laughed harshly. "I, on the other hand, have plenty to say. Mostly about you not performing your duty."

"Explain yourself, Jace," Paul demanded. Dan's face whitened, although he remained defiant.

Not removing his hard gaze from Dan, Jace responded.

"Lieutenant Willis was instructed to remain on guard duty until another officer relieved him. Instead, I arrived to find that he had abandoned his post and someone had started a fire in the kitchen. Miss Swanson was barricaded in her bathroom, ice-cold and going into shock." He smiled, a hard smile completely without humor.

Dan sneered. "I called Sergeant Thompson before going. He said he would cover for me."

"I see." Paul narrowed his eyes at the defiant officer. "And what was so important that it couldn't even wait until the other officer arrived?"

Flushing, Dan darted nervous eyes between his colleagues. "I had some personal business, sir."

"You left your charge because you had personal business, Lieutenant? Am I hearing you correctly? Because if harm had come to Miss Swanson, it would have been on your head."

Dan entered the room and settled his furious glare on the slender girl on the couch. Satisfaction flitted across his face when she noticed him and gasped in fright.

"I don't want him here!" Melanie's fierce whisper brought a frown to both Jace's and Paul's faces.

Paul walked closer to the couch, hands out front as though he was approaching a wounded animal. His gaze never left her wary face. Jace felt himself tense as he watched the interaction. He could practically feel Melanie's fear from where he stood.

Her wide brown eyes sought out Jace. He felt ridiculously pleased that she instinctively turned to him for reassurance. He nodded to her. She turned back to the chief.

"Ma'am," the chief continued, his voice as soothing as a summer breeze, "has Lieutenant Willis acted inappropriately? Besides abandoning you, of course."

Jace couldn't stop a snide grin from sliding across his

face at Paul's comments. Apparently the chief wasn't any more impressed with the man than he was. His smile widened as Dan's face reddened like a ripe tomato.

Melanie hesitated. The men held their breath. Finally she shrugged. "Just a remark or two."

Paul nodded.

"Go wait in the car, Dan."

"What? Are you really going to let that little—" Dan's enraged voice echoed off the walls. His fists were clenched and he took another step toward Melanie. She cringed.

"Lieutenant Willis, out!" Paul bellowed.

Jace watched as Dan stormed out, colliding into the paramedics who were just entering the house.

His angry voice could be heard as he stalked to the cruiser and got in, slamming the door.

For a few seconds, those inside the house stood in awkward silence. Then the paramedic team moved to their patient on the couch. Paul left to confer with the fire chief. Jace cast a quick glance at Melanie to be sure she was all right. Her eyes were closed and she was pale, but the paramedics seemed to have everything under control as they checked her vitals. Satisfied, he went after Paul.

He found the chief starring at the stove in disbelief. Years of practice allowed him to focus on the matter at hand, even when memories of finding Melanie, cold and unresponsive, threatened to intrude. He had been wrong to think that the attacker was just toying with her. It was clear now that whoever was behind all of this wanted her dead. But why? And how was it connected to the death of Alayna Brown? It seemed that there was more to Melanie's trial and conviction than met the eye. Doubt about her culpability in the death of the young woman four years before was growing stronger. If he wanted to find the truth, though, he needed to be the best cop he was capable of being.

"The fire chief said this looked like an ordinary kitchen fire. He sees this all the time. People never seem to realize how dangerous it could be to leave grease on the stove," Paul mused.

"If I hadn't come here, it would have looked like an accident," Jace affirmed. "But, Paul, I was here for breakfast just this morning. Sarah Swanson didn't have a can of grease on the stove. I'm sure of it."

"Then this was staged."

Jace nodded. "That's my take on it."

"Are you thinking that Dan had anything to do with this?" Paul asked. He held up his hand before Jace could answer. "Leave your emotions out of this, Jace. I don't want to disrupt the department any more than necessary."

Jace considered the facts. The man was rude and incompetent, but a criminal? He just couldn't see it. Slowly, he shook his head. "I don't know, Paul. I think he is prejudiced. He might even have a bit of a mean streak in him. I don't have enough evidence yet, though, to accuse him of anything more than neglecting his duty. And—" his voice hardened "—endangering the life of a civilian."

"I agree. I am hesitant to relieve him from duty. There's too little information for that. He will receive a formal reprimand. Let's keep an eye on him." Paul narrowed his eyes and looked at the ruined stove and the scorched cupboards above it. "Something is bugging me, but I can't quite put my finger on it."

Jace nodded. He had the same feeling. "There's something else," Jace stated. "Remember how I was searching for that car that nearly ran Melanie over at the hospital? I don't think that was a reckless kid anymore. I think Melanie was deliberately targeted. Someone wants her dead."

Melanie gritted her teeth as the paramedics checked her blood pressure. Of all the rotten luck! Could this day get any worse? Now Seth was here smirking as he removed the blood pressure cuff from her arm. When he reached for her wrist to check her pulse, she barely kept herself from pulling her arm from his grasp. Judging from the glance he threw her, he knew she hated having him touch her. And her reaction amused him.

"You're fine, Melanie. Get some food. Keep warm."

"Good. You can go now."

Seth clucked his tongue in disappointment. "Is that any way to treat an old friend, honey?"

Melanie grimaced. The other paramedic was trying not to gawk at them, but she was failing pathetically. When Mel gave a gusty sigh, the paramedic smiled and winked at her. Surprised, Mel smiled back. It was a relief to meet someone who didn't hate her on sight.

Brisk footsteps alerted her to Jace's return. It was embarrassing how aware of him she was. She thought she would probably recognize his confident stride anywhere. Not to mention the appealing scent of his woodsy aftershave as he came to stand next to her. She was confused by how his presence both calmed and unsettled her. She was a bundle of contradictions.

"How's the patient?" His soft voice was a warm blanket around her sore heart.

Seth smirked. "She's gonna be just fine, aren't you, honey?"

No, no, no. This was so not happening now. She nearly groaned out loud at the look of disbelief on Jace's face before he schooled his features into his "cop face."

"I told you not to call me that," she barked at Seth. When his smirk widened, she decided that ignoring him was her best choice. "We grew up together."

Please, please let him leave it at that. Of course, she doubted Seth would be able to do that. He was too fond of stirring up trouble. She suspected that that was why he'd dated her in the first place—because his father disapproved. At the time, though, she'd been foolish enough to believe they were in love.

Seth laughed. It was an ugly little sound. Really, how could she have once thought it was attractive?

"We not only grew up together—until four years ago, we were engaged."

Mortification filled her at the shock on Jace's face. This time, she did groan. Immediately both men turned their attention back to her. Seth's snarky attitude faded as he did his job. As much as she couldn't stand the man anymore, he was an outstanding paramedic.

"Head hurting?" he queried.

Melanie started to nod, then thought better of it. The pain throbbed behind her eyes. Her head suddenly felt as if it weighed a ton. She closed her eyes. Vaguely she was aware that the two men were talking about her. She was in too much agony to care.

"Stress headache," Seth declared. "She doesn't get 'em a lot. But when she does, it's a doozy."

"Can you give her something?" Jace bit out.

"Yeah, but she won't like it. Mel, come on, girl. You need to take this. Open your eyes."

Melanie opened her eyes to find Seth holding a couple of tablets in his hand. Jace appeared with a glass of water. She felt bile rising in her throat even before she tried to swallow the medication. She moaned. Partly in pain, partly in protest. Her heart pounded at the idea of trying to swallow the pills. She knew from past experience what would happen.

"Can't!" she managed to gasp.

"Melanie, you're in pain. You need to take something for relief," Jace coaxed her.

She swung her gaze to Seth. "He…doesn't…understand."

"I know. But it might help." Seth reached out and grabbed the small wastebasket that was beside the couch. He set it on the floor in front of her. "Look, I'm prepared if it doesn't work."

Jace looked as if he wanted to say something, but wasn't sure what. His expression had grown more confused with every word. Mel was too distraught to explain it to him. Anyway, she was pretty sure he would understand the problem as soon as she swallowed.

Grabbing the water and one tablet, she did her best to comply. Unfortunately, her best wasn't enough. As soon as she tried to swallow, her gag reflex kicked in. It was a fearsome thing to behold. All her life she had suffered with it. She couldn't breathe. Her throat contracted and she retched. Again and again. Tears spilled down her cheeks. She flailed her arms, knowing she needed the wastebasket. Jace dove for it. He held it under her face just as she vomited. Spent, she lay back, panting.

"Does this happen every time you take pills?" Jace demanded, his face bewildered.

"Every single time." Seth answered for her, his cocky tone gone. "She normally tries children's chewables, but I don't have any."

"Maybe her aunt has some."

"I looked in the medicine cabinet, before…" Melanie's voice faded away as exhaustion took its toll.

"Why didn't you just tell me?" Jace demanded of Seth.

"I guess I keep hoping she will have grown out of it. It's something you see in children. I have never seen another adult with a gag reflex like hers."

In the silence that followed, only Mel's soft hiccoughs could be heard.

"What I would like to know," Chief Kennedy's soft voice broke the stillness, "is how this young lady could have possibly attempted to commit suicide by swallowing half a bottle of prescription medication?"

A startled hush fell over the room.

"There were no needle marks, so it wasn't by injection," Chief Kennedy mused, one hand cupping his chin. "I guess it's possible that she could have crushed the pills and mixed them with liquid. The lab report did say there was alcohol in her system."

Melanie snorted. Then groaned. Jace touched her shoulder, but his attention was focused on Chief Kennedy.

"Not likely, Chief," he asserted. "The pills were scattered around her. She was lying in a bed, without anything to crush the pills against. The pill bottle was even in her palm. It was made to look like she had been holding the bottle as she drifted off."

"Made to look? Jace, are you implying someone set her up?" Chief Kennedy's quiet question set Melanie's heart racing. Was it possible Jace was starting to believe her?

"I have been telling people for four years now that I didn't try to kill myself," Melanie murmured.

"Yes, but you couldn't explain what had happened. And you can't deny the drugs were in your system," Jace responded.

"I know the drugs were in my system." She opened her eyes slightly to glare at him. The effort was too exhausting, so they drifted shut again. "My throat hurt for three days because of that nasty tube they shoved down it to pump out my stomach. I just can't tell you how it happened. I'm thinking that many drugs messes with a person's memory."

Jace turned his icy gaze on the paramedic. "You knew she couldn't swallow pills, and you said nothing? What kind of fiancé were you?"

"Hey!" An indignant expression crossed the young man's face. "We weren't engaged anymore. We had broken up two months earlier. I wasn't even in the country. I was spending my last year of university as an exchange student in Paris."

Melanie huffed in annoyance.

"What?" Seth demanded.

"We didn't break up. Your father was embarrassed by my family and you went along with him. You signed up for that program, then dropped me. We had been best friends for years, you had asked me to *marry* you, but you totally abandoned me. You never even tried to communicate with me after I was arrested, which really helped me prove my innocence."

Seth flushed, looking embarrassed for the first time. His eyes shifted to his feet. "I didn't know what to do. My father was running for the senate. His opponent was digging up as much dirt on him as he could—"

"And your father considered me 'dirt.'"

Seth had the grace to look embarrassed.

Jace's lip curled as he looked at Seth. Her good humor was restored slightly to know that Jace was irritated on her behalf.

A sharp rap on the door frame caught their attention. "Yoo-hoo! Can anyone join this party?"

They looked up to see a bubbly blonde, around fifty with a kind face and a sharp designer suit, at the door. She glided into the room on a cloud of heavy perfume. For the first time in hours, Melanie smiled.

"Cathy! There's always room for you."

Cathy sashayed over and leaned down to give Mel a kiss on her cheek. Mel held her breath until Cathy moved away. She liked Cathy, but she didn't want an asthma attack right now.

Mel grinned to herself when she heard Jace mutter to Seth, "We're not done. You will hear from me."

"Why am I not surprised?" Seth grumbled.

"I never expected to see you!" Melanie gestured toward the woman as she made the introductions. "Cathy Jordan was my defense attorney and surrogate mother during the trial. She did her best."

Cathy smiled at the greeting. "I heard you were here, and about your poor aunt! Thought I'd stop by and see if you needed anything." Cathy stopped talking and sniffed, a confused expression crossing her face. "What is that awful smell?"

Melanie waved her hand in a negligent manner. "Oh, I had a small fire in the kitchen. It's out, but the place might smell for a day or two."

Jace gave her a swift glance. She shook her head. Though they hadn't known each other before Cathy had agreed to represent Melanie during the trial, Cathy had become one of her dearest friends. She was the only person besides her aunt to visit her in prison. Yet for some reason, Melanie was reluctant to tell her what happened.

"Well, I'm glad you weren't hurt, Mel. Oh, I almost forgot!" Cathy said in her North Carolina drawl, handing a large brown envelope to Melanie. "This was lying on your front porch."

SEVEN

Melanie drew back against the couch. From the look on her face, Cathy might as well have been holding a cobra. It was clear there was no way she was going to touch it, so Jace took charge. Extracting the envelope from Melanie's grasp, he jerked his head toward the den. Paul nodded. Using his radio, he asked Sergeant Olsen to report to the house. As soon as the eager young sergeant arrived, Paul ordered him to remain with Melanie until he was told otherwise.

Jace was torn. On the one hand, Miles was so young, "wet behind the ears" as his father used to say. Jace doubted if the kid had ever even drawn his service weapon. On the other hand, he knew that Miles was tougher than he looked. The kid had a black belt. What had cinched it, though, was when Paul had pointed out that Dan was the only other policeman on scene. Jace followed Paul to the den.

After shutting the door, he opened the envelope and withdrew the contents—which were just what he had expected. More pictures. He and Melanie at the front door that morning. Leaving in the car. The hospital. There was a sheet of paper with another message in cutout letters. This one read HE CAN'T PROTECT YOU. LEAVE TOWN OR FACE THE CONSEQUENCES.

"This needs to stop," Jace ground out, his rage almost tangible. He thrust the offensive pictures and note back into the envelope, shoved them into Paul's hands and started to pace the length of Sarah Swanson's den. He was careful to keep his voice low so that it would not carry into the next room where Melanie and Cathy were still talking over the day's events.

"I agree," Paul concurred. "What's your next step?" He leaned against the desk.

Jace stopped pacing and glared out the window. He rubbed one hand through his close-cropped hair, frustration gnawing at him. What *was* the next step? He was positive Melanie was being targeted. He wasn't sure why or by whom. The only thing he was sure of was that it was all somehow tied to the case four years ago.

"I need to finish questioning the rest of the jurors from Mel's trial. I drove to Grove City this morning and talked with one. That leaves ten more," he mused aloud. "I also want to review the evidence and all the old case notes. I'm missing something."

"You could assign someone else to call them, make the process go quicker."

Jace was shaking his head before Paul finished speaking. "No, not this time. I want to see the jurors' reaction to Melanie. It's a long shot, but maybe their reactions will tell me something. They may be afraid to say if they were threatened."

Paul snapped open his cell phone and dialed the station. He ordered the requested information and files to be located and made available to Jace immediately. He also requested that the information be kept secure. Only he or Jace would be allowed to peruse it. Jace raised an eyebrow at Paul. Although he appreciated the precautions, they were not the standard for the small-town police station.

"Something more on your mind, Chief?"

Paul shrugged. "I don't want to take any chances. And I definitely don't want Dan getting any more involved with this case than necessary. I checked on his story, and he did ask Sergeant Thompson to cover. Unfortunately, Thompson's wife went into labor and he left for the hospital. He forgot to mention to the operator that someone was needed here. Be that as it may, Dan should have waited until his backup arrived. He has some kind of bee in his bonnet about Miss Swanson. He is reacting to her too personally." Then Paul narrowed his steely gaze on his lieutenant. Jace resisted the impulse to squirm. "So are you, old friend. I don't want you to mess things up by becoming too involved. Jace? Are you hearing me?"

Aggravated, Jace sighed. He barely resisted the urge to roll his eyes. "Too late for that, Paul. I am involved, and have been for four years. But I am not backing out of this case. It's mine. And if Melanie is innocent, then I owe it to her to prove it. I am the one who built the case that sent her to jail in the first place." He thrust out his chin, daring Paul to pull him off the case. This time, badge or not, he would not let Melanie down.

"It appears the suicide attempt was bogus." Paul stroked his chin, apparently deep in thought. "Tell me what else bothers you."

Jace started ticking off facts on his fingers. "Sylvie and Melanie had made plans to meet that day. Someone at the college, another student, had seen Melanie exiting the elevator on Sylvie's floor the day of the murder. Melanie's driver's license was found at the crime scene. And there was the suicide note claiming she had sold the girl bad heroin, which killed Sylvie. That obviously was false if the suicide attempt was staged."

Jace resumed pacing. "No one ever found any physical evidence of Melanie in the dorm room where Sylvie was found. No hair, no fingerprints, nothing."

"I remember that. I thought perhaps she had worn gloves."

"Yeah, but remember how we thought it was really strange that she had fingerprints on the outside of the door? If she had been smart enough to wear gloves inside, why not at the door? And why, if she was smart enough to have worn gloves, would she have taken out her driver's license?"

"Thoughts?" Paul said.

"I think she interrupted something. Maybe witnessed the murder. The killer drugged her, too, in hopes of killing her, and set her up with the suicide note to take the fall for Sylvie's death." Jace uttered the idea that had started growing in his mind. "I think whoever killed Sylvie was responsible for the threats against the jurors. But now at least one juror decided to come forward. And was murdered. I think the killer is getting nervous. Trying to get rid of anything or anyone that links him to the case, or that would cast doubt on Melanie's conviction."

"But why go to the trouble of making the attack on Melanie look like an accident?"

"Because as far as anyone knows, she is still the only suspect."

Frustrated, Jace rubbed his hands over his face. What was he supposed to do? Let some nutcase kill Melanie? Because that's what would happen if he stepped back. He was dead certain about that. He should have listened to his gut the first time around.

A strong hand clasped his shoulder. Jace turned back

to Paul, his cop mask once again in place. On the outside. Inside, his emotions churned. Paul was a real stickler for keeping the department's image spotless. Now that he could see how much this case—this woman—meant to Jace, it was very likely he would order Jace off the case. Maybe even suggest he take some vacation time. Jace had never disobeyed Paul's directives. He knew how jealous some of the other officers were of his friendship with the chief and was careful to never ask for special treatment. This time, however, was different. Jace would not be able to calmly step aside and let some less experienced officer, one who might think Melanie got what she deserved, take his case. No way.

"Fine. I'll let you stay on the case," Paul stated. Jace blinked, sure he had misunderstood. "You have never let me down before, so I will trust you now. But I am warning you, Jace, I don't want this to hurt the department in any way."

"It won't," Jace promised.

"All right, then. Next question. She can't remain here. I want her closer to town. That way we can get to her quicker without spreading ourselves too thin. Any suggestions?"

"Yeah," Jace drawled.

"You care to share?"

"I thought I'd take her to meet my mom."

"It's a little baggy, but it'll do." Mel scrutinized her reflection in her aunt's bedroom mirror. When Jace had demanded in his most authoritative voice that she pack a bag for several days, she had pulled Cathy into her room with her while she searched for clothing that still fit her. Or at least wouldn't fall off. Never a large woman, her thin frame now appeared almost skeletal. She didn't care for that at all.

"How long do you think you'll be gone?" Cathy inquired as she wandered the room, stopping every now and then to pick up a book or examine a photo.

Melanie shrugged, putting another outfit in the open suitcase on the bed. "I don't have a clue. Jace said it could be several days. Maybe even a week. He is really concerned that someone might be out to get me."

Cathy flashed her a look that clearly said, "Duh...do ya think so?"

"Oh, don't give me that look."

Light laughter spilled from Cathy's painted pink mouth. "Oh, now, honey. Don't go getting yourself into a flutter! If I had a handsome man like that getting all protective on me, I'd be lapping it up."

"Cathy, there's nothing personal about it..."

The older woman rolled her eyes. Melanie flushed. There had been something very personal about the way Jace had watched her walk out of the room, and she knew it. Just as she knew that Seth had not been happy to leave. His scowl at Jace as he left was a clear indication of that. Not that Mel would ever take Seth seriously again. He had broken more than her heart when he'd abandoned her four years ago. He had destroyed her trust, too.

"Yoo-hoo. Melanie, sweetie? Where did you go?"

Melanie blinked. She had been so lost in her thoughts, she had completely forgotten Cathy's presence and their errand.

"Sorry, Cath. Did you say something?"

"I was just thinking out loud, that's all. Wondering why someone would be after you now."

Head tilted, Mel pondered the question. "I've thought about that. I think maybe whoever really killed Sylvie is afraid that I might remember something."

Eyes wide, Cathy whispered, "You really think it was

deliberate? That poor thing dying? Honey, you were not accused of murder, but manslaughter. That means it wasn't premeditated."

Melanie slammed the lid shut on her suitcase and latched it with a single fierce twist.

"I'm not talking about me. You do believe me that I had nothing to do with her death, right?"

"Of course," Cathy answered, just a shade too quickly. She waved her hands as if erasing the subject. "Anyway, how likely is it that your memory will return? It's been four years."

"I know how long it's been," she said quietly, forcing herself not to snap. "But I have really hazy memories of that night. I remember standing outside a door, but after that, it's all a blur. Who knows? Maybe I will remember as time goes on."

"Honey, that would be great," Cathy gushed. "So where is Jace taking you, anyway?" Melanie opened her mouth, than closed it again. She couldn't quite explain it, but she was hesitant to say any more. Not that Cathy would ever do anything malicious. Oh, sure, she was a bit too sweet with all her *honeys* and *sweeties*. But she had stood beside Mel when no one else would. Melanie had been blessed when Cathy offered to become her defense attorney. Over the years, she had become more than Melanie's lawyer; she had become her friend. But still, Melanie had learned very well that one had to be cautious.

She lifted her shoulders in a noncommittal shrug. "Jace didn't say," she answered truthfully. "I need to grab my spare inhaler." Walking over to the night table, she grabbed it out of the top drawer.

"Oops!"

Melanie peered over her shoulder. And rolled her eyes. Cathy had knocked Melanie's purse off the bed, spilling its contents. The blonde was shoveling the items back inside the canvas bag at full speed. "Sorry, hon. You know I can be klutzy." She handed the purse back to Melanie.

"Thanks." Melanie swung the bag over her shoulder. Grabbing the handle of the suitcase, she hefted it with one hand, then led the way back to where the men were waiting.

An hour later, Jace pulled into the police station and shut off the motor. Mel half expected him to order her to remain in the car while he went inside, but instead he motioned for her to follow him. They headed toward the main door, but stopped when Senator Travis barreled out, red-faced. He saw Jace and headed in his direction.

"Someone get me a red flag," Mel muttered under her breath. She cut her eyes up at Jace. Uh-oh. Judging by the way his lips were twitching, he had heard her.

He confirmed it when he replied sotto voce, "Toro!"

"Lieutenant Tucker," the senator roared, coming to a stop mere inches from them. Mel almost stepped back, but a discreet tug on her wrist told her to stand her ground.

"Senator Travis," Jace said, stone-faced.

The senator looked down his nose at Melanie. "You, leave us alone. I need to speak with the lieutenant on important business."

"Sorry, Senator. Miss Swanson and I are busy. Whatever business you have can be handled by another officer."

The senator seemed to swell before their eyes. "I don't want another officer! You have a reputation of being very thorough. I need you to look into the break-ins at my home and office."

"You didn't mention your office before," Jace rapped out.

The older man gave Melanie a distrustful scowl. "That's

because I only noticed it today. Someone went through my desk. Messed up all my files. Broke several pictures. I think my opponent is searching for dirt."

"Sir, I will look into it. I promise. I will send several officers out today to document the damage, and I will follow up later."

Lips twisting, the senator nodded. "I guess I'll have to be satisfied with that for now." He started to walk away, yelling back over his shoulder. "If I were you, son, I'd tell your boss you want to ditch the ex-con. Hang out with her kind and bad things are likely to happen."

In a flash, Jace's cool facade melted. Furious, he stalked to the senator. "Are you threatening me, Senator Travis?"

"Whoa, easy now. You're getting mighty riled over some friendly advice." The senator raised his hands and backed away, a knowing smile crossing his face. He twisted his neck to sneer at Melanie. "You may have this young lieutenant here fooled, but I remember your father, girl. The apple didn't fall far from the tree, as they say. You and your old man, rotten on the inside."

Mel touched Jace's arm as he stiffened beside her. "Let it go, Jace."

The senator departed, whistling.

Blowing out a frustrated breath, Jace resumed heading into the police station. "Let's finish here and go."

Jace left her waiting in a conference room while he gathered the files. He was gone for half an hour. When he finally came to get her, he was carrying several thick document envelopes. As she caught sight of him, her eyes widened. He had changed clothes while he was inside. Melanie could hardly keep her eyes off the man coming toward her. Gone was the stern lieutenant focused on his duty. In his place stood a relaxed man dressed in faded blue jeans, a red flannel shirt and dusty cowboy boots. Mel half expected him to pull out a cowboy hat.

"I've got what I need," he stated, hefting the envelopes slightly. "Let's motor."

She wanted to ask him what he'd found, but one glance at him told her his mind was on other things. She didn't mind. It was pleasant to walk beside him and just *be*. She waited until he unlocked his cruiser, than started to get in.

"Nope." Jace hefted her suitcase out of the backseat and shut the door. He waited until she had stepped up beside him, then relocked the doors. "I'm leaving the cruiser here." Pivoting on his heel, Jace led the way to a blue Ford pickup truck. He politely opened her door for her, giving her a mock bow as he motioned her to climb inside. She had never seen him so lighthearted before.

She was fascinated by the change in him as they drove out of the parking lot. So fascinated that she almost missed the ludicrous suggestion he was making when he told her where they were going. Lieutenant Jace Tucker, a pillar of the community and an all-around righteous man, wanted to take her, a convicted felon, to stay with his mother. She didn't know his mom, but she was pretty sure that idea would go over like a lead balloon.

"Jace, your mom is not going to want me to go to her house," she protested.

"It's the only place where I can keep you safe," he replied, his jaw tightening in the stubborn way she was becoming used to. They argued for several moments. Finally, Mel sat back with a huff. Unexpectedly, Jace chuckled. She glared in response. That only seemed to amuse him even more.

"I'm sorry, Mel, but you are just too cute when you get all snippy."

"Snippy!"

"Yep. Snippy."

There was no answer to that. Without thinking, she reached out and clicked the radio on. And received yet another surprising glimpse of Jace. Expecting country music, she found herself listening to Mozart instead. Her amazed glance flew to his flushed face.

"Classical? You listen to classical?" She couldn't keep the amazement from her voice.

"Yeah. The guys here like to rib me about it. They all listen to country." He rubbed a hand across the back of his neck "I play the piano, too."

Finding something they had in common, she forgot where they were going. For the next fifteen minutes, they compared opinions on composers and various interpretations. It wasn't until Jace slowed down before a blue ranch-style house that Mel remembered their destination.

Jace shrugged. He pulled into his mother's house and turned off the engine. They sat quietly for a few moments before he abruptly opened the door and stepped out of the truck. "Come on, Mel. Let's not keep my mom waiting."

Reluctantly, Mel followed him up the short walkway. Her stomach tightened when a woman opened the door. Her blue eyes were identical to Jace's, except for the generous smattering of laugh lines fanning them. Only she wasn't laughing now. Or even smiling. In fact, her expression was cold and remote. She took in Mel's appearance the same way one might view a bug found in their salad. Her eyes stayed on Mel while she greeted her son and tilted her face for a kiss.

"Take her upstairs. The guest room is ready." Mel shivered. This was just about the most uncomfortable welcome she had ever had into anyone's home.

"Sure, Mom. I'm starving. Is it okay if I make us something to eat?" Jace's cheerful tone was forced.

"I'm not sure what I have in the kitchen. I didn't feel like going shopping today. You'll have to fend for yourselves tonight."

Well, now. That was clear enough. Jace paused on his way toward the stairs and frowned at his mother. Whatever he wanted to say, though, he kept to himself. Mel was just as glad. She didn't want to be the cause of any more friction in this family.

"Jace!" A lovely young woman with auburn hair ran into the room to embrace him. She looked several years younger than Jace. Her high cheekbones and blue eyes immediately identified her as his sister. Mel tensed when the pretty woman turned to greet her. Then her mouth fell open as the woman sent her a friendly smile. "You must be Jace's friend Melanie. I'm his sister, Irene."

Mrs. Tucker snorted when Irene called Mel Jace's friend. The other three tactfully ignored her.

"You mean my pesky sister, don't you, Brat?" Jace playfully tugged a hank of Irene's hair. The affectionate gesture made a lump form in Melanie's throat. She missed being around people who genuinely cared for her. As horrible as the prison had been, she at least had the chaplain and two other inmates who had joined her at the prison church services.

Jace turned and began walking toward the stairs again. "Come on, Mel. Let's get you settled, then we'll go grab a bite to eat."

Gratefully, Mel hurried after him. The less time she spent in this house, the better.

"Hey, what about me?" Irene yelled after them.

"What about you?" Jace shot back. "You have your own family to feed at home. We'll catch up with you later."

"Fine, fine. I know when I'm not wanted. I'll talk with you later. Nice meeting you, Melanie." Irene fluttered her fingers at them, kissed her mother's disapproving cheek and waltzed out the door.

Mel started in astonishment when Jace grabbed her hand and pulled her up the stairs and down the hall to the spare bedroom. He opened the door and motioned her inside. Instead of following her inside, he stood in the doorway. They stared at each other for a few moments. The air almost vibrated with tension. Finally he nodded.

"Right. You grab a shower and a change of clothes. We can leave in about thirty minutes." He started to shut the door, then paused. "It will all work out, Mel. Trust me," he promised, his voice soft and smooth as velvet.

Emotion clogged her throat. She couldn't have answered him if she wanted to. She settled for a brief nod. As soon as he shut the door, she sagged down onto the bed. Her head drooped into her hands.

It was closer to forty minutes by the time she felt brave enough to venture out of the room and seek out Jace. She'd procrastinated as long as she could. The thought that finally motivated her to leave her sanctuary was that she didn't want to add to Mrs. Tucker's already dismal impression of her.

She heard Jace before she saw him. He and his mother were in the kitchen. It was apparent by the tone of his mother's voice that they were arguing. As she drew closer, the words became clearer. She intended to make her presence immediately known, but hearing her name stopped her.

"Melanie has nowhere else to go, Mom." Jace's voice was calm, but Mel could hear the underlying tension.

"So? How is that your problem?" Mrs. Tucker snarled.

Jace sighed. "Mom, it is my duty to protect her. Someone is after her."

A sound like something being slammed on the counter

echoed through the room. Mel flinched. "I can't believe you, Jason Tucker! How could you bring that...that...that drug dealer into my home!"

"Mom..."

"No! It's not right. Her kind has caused us so much pain. Or have you forgotten? Have you let a pretty face blind you? I can't imagine what made you think you could bring her here after what happened to Ellie." The last word broke on a sob.

Mel shuddered. Her heart ached for the woman. Ellie. That must have been the other sister Jace had mentioned. Right before he froze her out at breakfast. Although she didn't know all the details, Mel was pretty sure that his little sister was dead, and that drugs were somehow involved. No wonder the woman was unhappy about having Melanie in her home. How could she stay here and add to that mother's agony? Mrs. Tucker had no reason to doubt that Mel was guilty.

At the same time, she wanted to scream that she wasn't a drug dealer. Her jaw tensed and she clenched her fists at her sides as frustration beat at her. As wild as she had been in her teens, she had never touched drugs—not to use them or to sell them. But for the rest of her life, people would think she had.

"Mom, please," Jace entreated. "I know it's hard to accept. But Melanie isn't what you think."

What? Was Jace defending her? It was one thing for him to stand up for her to Lieutenant Willis or Dan. But to his heartbroken mother? But maybe he was just trying to pacify his mother. Still, she had trouble picturing him lying to anyone, especially his mother, to make things easier.

"How can you say that? You were the one who arrested her," came the tear-filled reply.

Melanie had heard enough. She stepped through the

doorway. Both people in the kitchen froze at her entrance. She was vaguely aware of Jace's weary expression. She focused on the devastated woman standing at the counter, wet coffee stains on her blouse. Ah. She must have slammed her coffee mug on the counter and it splashed. The woman's drawn face tugged at Mel's heart.

"I won't stay here if it bothers you that much, Mrs. Tucker," she murmured. Jace opened his mouth, but Mel held up a hand to halt him.

"I can stay in a hotel. You did try to convince me to do that before, remember? Your mother shouldn't have to let someone into her house she doesn't like."

Jace stalked over to Mel, glaring. "But she doesn't know all the facts," he insisted, teeth gritted.

"Neither do you," she pointed out.

"I know that I was wrong not following my instincts four years ago," he declared.

EIGHT

"What are you saying?" Her voice was a mere whisper.

Jace cleared his throat. He rubbed the back of his head. It was never comfortable to admit you were wrong, but he needed to man up. "I should not say this. It's unprofessional, but I owe it to you after what I've done." He paused. Looked into her eyes. "I don't think you killed that girl, nor do I believe you tried to kill yourself. I felt I was missing something back then, and the events in the past couple of days have clinched it for me. I think you were framed. It's quite possible you were the victim of an attempted murder, as well."

A pregnant silence filled the room.

"If you felt I was innocent," she managed to rasp, "why didn't you ever say so? Why did you work so hard to build the case against me?"

Jace began to pace the length of the small room.

"All the evidence I had pointed to you. I couldn't ignore that. But I wasn't comfortable with the fact that all the evidence was circumstantial. And there was something about you… I didn't want to think that you could be a killer. It just didn't seem to fit. But I told myself I had to be wrong, that I couldn't value a gut feeling over all the evidence. At one point, I even considered asking Paul to remove me from your case." He lifted one shoulder in a shrug. "After you were convicted, I made myself believe you had to have been guilty. The jury came back so quickly, as if they had no doubt at all. I was astonished, but I told myself it was because you were so obviously guilty—that I was the one who was wrong for not seeing it. It almost wrecked my career."

"*She* almost wrecked your career," Mrs. Tucker reminded her son. "People who deal in drugs will lie about anything. Just look what happened to your sister."

"Mom…"

"No! I went to church with her parents. They appeared decent, but the whole time that man was abusing drugs and his wife and child."

He couldn't help the way his mouth dropped open. He whipped his head in Mel's direction. Even if he had doubted his mother, the slump of her shoulders and the down-turned gaze told him his mother was right.

"Mel?"

She flinched.

"Go ahead and ask her how they died. Well? Ask her. In my mind she was destined to turn out bad from the get-go."

"Mom, the reports on her parents' death said there was a car crash. And as far as the other, everyone I interviewed had nothing but praise."

"You obviously didn't interview Melanie's teachers at school. I was teaching then. I could tell you stories that would horrify you. Or what about Mrs. Johns, who lived across the street from the Swanson family? If she were still alive, she could tell you a thing or two about what went on in that family."

"Mom, what about forgiveness? Grace? Don't you believe in any of that?"

Mrs. Tucker refused to meet his eyes. "I thought I did.

But now, faced with her presence in my home, I don't know." She shook her head and walked to the door. "I will allow her to stay tonight, since you told your chief you were bringing her here. Tomorrow, though, you need to find her somewhere else."

Grief filled him as he watched his mother's proud figure march from the room. He had thought—well, he didn't know what he had thought. Being an honest man, who had taken an oath to protect and serve this community, he needed to find out if Mel had been a victim, too. It was the right thing to do. He had known his mother wouldn't be happy about having Mel in her house, but he never thought she'd turn her out. A prickle of unease settled in his gut. What was he supposed to do now?

"She's right, you know." Mel stood beside him, sadness stamped on her weary face. "I want to show you something. Hold on." Mel went and collected her purse. Dropping it on the table, she began to riffle through its contents. "I know it's here. Oh, Cathy, what have you done?" she muttered.

"What are you looking for?"

"I'm searching for—hey! Here it is." She fished a small wallet out of the bag.

"You might want to organize that thing," he said mildly.

"It was organized," she retorted, "until Cathy knocked it over. Who knows what is still lying on the floor back at Aunt Sarah's house." She opened the wallet and showed him a picture of a young woman. She was an older version of Mel. She was beautiful, but there was something haunted about her expression.

"Your mom?" he guessed.

"Yes. It's the only picture of her I have."

"You don't have a picture of your dad?" Before the question was finished, her mouth had flattened, tightened.

"My father was an evil man. He went to church every week, and everyone loved him. Then he'd come home, and…well, it wasn't pretty."

"What happened, Mel?"

"He killed her," she said bluntly. "Maybe deliberately, maybe not. But it was his fault, just the same. He was high, and he drove their car onto the train tracks and stopped as a train was coming. Witnesses said they could see Mom trying to escape, but he held her in the car."

Bile churned in his gut. What kind of creature did that? Another thought struck him.

"Where were you?"

Her hands clenched at her side. He could see her throat moving as she swallowed. Her eyes darted to his, then away.

"Home."

"With?"

She shrugged. "Myself. Dad thought I was a nuisance. No fun to have a ten-year-old kid around."

"Mel—"

Ignoring him, she continued talking, almost as if she were talking to herself. "I really can't blame people for distrusting me. And whoever set me up did it well. Looking at the situation objectively, I think it would be hard to convince anyone I didn't hurt Sylvie. I was rather wild in my teens. I hung out with the wrong kids. I never did drugs, or even alcohol, because I couldn't stand the taste of the stuff, but—"

"That's it! That's what I was missing!" Jace dashed out of the room to get the files he'd retrieved from the police station. He hurried back in a minute later, leafing through a file until he found what he was looking for. He grabbed a paper and waved it at Melanie.

"Here it is! Mel, when your stomach was pumped at

the hospital, there were large quantities of alcohol in your system, along with the pills. When I swept your apartment for evidence, I found the suicide note that you had supposedly written, and the bottle of prescription painkillers we assumed you had stolen from Seth. Some pills strewn over the floor. Like you'd been in a hurry. Dropped them. But there was no alcohol, or even empty bottles, anywhere on the premises."

"Of course not," Mel sniffed. "I don't drink."

He waved the file at her. "But don't you see? If you had really overdosed on painkillers *and* vodka, why didn't we find the bottle? Even if you had cleaned up after yourself, which you clearly didn't, hence the pills on the floor... even if you had, we would have found it somewhere. In the garbage or recycling. I *scoured* that apartment collecting evidence. Nothing."

He walked away, then whirled to face her. "There is no way that you could have done the deed in your apartment. Someone overdosed you, then put you there, spilling the pills all around you. It was probably a shock to whoever it was that you survived to stand trial. Of course, your memory lapse helped them since you couldn't identify who had done this to you. But they had to make sure no one had any doubt that you were solely responsible for Sylvie's death. That's why the jurors were threatened. That's why someone tried to kill your aunt Sarah. That's why someone is after you now. They need to clean up their mistakes." Jace grabbed hold of Mel's waist and whirled her around. Then he backed away, flushing. "Sorry. Got a little too enthusiastic."

"It's all right," Mel murmured, her expression stunned.

"We need a plan. But I can't do that until I eat. Let's order a pizza and then we can get our strategy worked out."

"Your mom?" Mel gestured vaguely toward the door.

"We'll go down to the basement. Shouldn't disturb her there. Hopefully, we can change her mind about you tomorrow."

Forty-five minutes later, they were seated together eating the best pizza Mel had ever tasted. Or maybe it was the company. Jace had shed some of his reserve in her presence. He even told her about his sister.

"Ellie was a sweet kid. Shy, tenderhearted. She was always the kid with her nose in a book. She also loved the Lord, and tried so hard to always do the right thing. She was so eager to make everyone happy—she never wanted to hurt or disappoint anyone." He paused while he took a gulp of his soda.

Mel found her eyes drawn to the strong column of his throat as he tilted his head back. She blushed when he set his drink down, thankful that he hadn't seen her staring.

He resumed talking. "When she was sixteen, we noticed a change. Not a huge one. She just started being more aware of how she looked, what she wore. We figured she probably had a crush on a boy. We were right." He frowned. "Jeff Marcus. He was a year older in school. Seemed like a nice kid. We met him. He was very polite, a good student. He used to come over and hang out with me while he waited for Ellie to finish getting ready. Sometimes he'd help me tinker on my motorcycle in the garage. He even joined Paul and me once when we went to Pittsburgh for a football game. I really liked that kid. It was like having a little brother. What I didn't know, what none of us knew, was that he sold drugs on the side."

Jace stopped and rubbed his eyes.

Mel reached over and touched the hand lying on the table. "Jace, you don't have to tell me. I understand."

Jace turned his hand over and grabbed on to hers as

though it was a lifeline. "I do need to tell you, Mel. I was unfair to you four years ago, and my mother was unfair to you today. You deserve to know why."

Her throat dry, she nodded for him to continue. If he needed to unburden himself, she would listen. There was no way she could turn her back on him when he was hurting.

"Jeff got my baby sister hooked on drugs. She died when she jumped out of a window while high."

He blew out a breath, hard. "Ellie called her best friend on her cell phone and left a voice mail for her right before she jumped. She said she was going to see if she could fly. They played that voice mail at Jeff's trial. Not a dry eye in the place. Jeff was convicted. He was tried as an adult since Ellie was a minor. But Ellie was gone."

"I am so sorry, Jace," Mel wept.

She doubted he even heard her.

"I was such a wreck after she died. How could I not have seen what had happened to her? If I'd noticed the signs, I could have gotten her help, treatment. I was her brother, the only father figure she had left. And I had failed her." He scorched her with the agony in his eyes. "I let affection for that boy cloud my judgment.

"Mel, when I saw Sylvie dead of an overdose, all I could see was Ellie. I'm ashamed to admit it, but Sylvie wasn't who I was fighting for, it was my sister. And fighting for her meant making sure the person responsible was put behind bars. I wanted to close the case—I wanted to go with the easy, obvious solution. So when I got that nagging feeling that something wasn't right, I tried to ignore it. I was disgusted with myself. I felt like I was having trouble doing my job."

Mel swallowed. "But surely you can't still blame yourself for the doubts about me anymore. You know you were right to question things, right?" She held her breath.

He let out a humorless chuckle. "*You* should be mad at me. Mel, do you realize that because I was such a jerk you lost four years of your life? Four years that you can never get back."

"Stop that!"

His head reared back at her sharp command. She lowered her voice.

"You know that part in the Old Testament, where Joseph meets his brothers years after they sold him as a slave?" She waited until he nodded. "Well, he told them that they might have meant to do something evil, but God took that and used it for good. That's what happened to me. I rejected my aunt's lessons about God, laughed at her faith and moved out at seventeen. I was living with Seth, and we were both thumbing our noses at his snobby parents and the rules of moral conduct we had learned. Then he broke up with me and two months later Sylvie died. When I went to jail, I was stripped of everything. My job, my home, my friends. Seth had already abandoned me, and his father was using every opportunity to denounce me. I was so bitter. Angry. That's when God showed me that He would never abandon me." She gestured around them at the posh decor of his mother's basement. "All of this is fleeting. Everything I had held dear was false. In jail, I learned that God was the only one I could depend on. Even if I marry someday, my husband will be a human who will make mistakes. So you see, Jace, you feel like you've cost me four years of my life. I feel like you've saved my soul."

A slice of pizza stopped halfway to his mouth, Jace's face reflected his astonishment.

A slight smile hovered about his handsome mouth.

"I'm glad you had faith to comfort you. It was the only

thing that kept us going when Ellie died." He cleared his throat and moved to a new topic.

"I want to go finish talking with the jurors tomorrow. Most of them are local. One moved out of state. I need to find the truth."

"You mean you are going to just leave me?"

He shook his head. "No. I already told Paul I was taking you with me. It's not normal procedure, but it would be safer for you."

She sighed, relieved. "Okay, whatever."

Later that night when Mel was getting ready for bed, there was a quiet knock on her door. She cast a glance down at her apparel and grimaced. Baggy sweats that had seen better days and a tie-dyed T-shirt with a heavy-metal rock band emblazoned across the front. Not exactly dressed to impress. She slipped her robe on to conceal the offending clothes, then walked on bare feet to the door. Pulling it open three inches, she peered out at Jace, who had his hand raised to knock again. She averted her eyes, trying not to smile as she noticed that he, too, was wearing old sweats and a T-shirt. Except his shirt featured Yoda from *Star Wars*.

"Yes?" she whispered, not wanting to remind his mother of her presence.

"I forgot to say…can you be ready by eight tomorrow morning? I'd really like to head out as soon as we can."

Her heart skipped a beat. A whole day driving around with Jace. She had mixed feelings about that. Excitement and nervousness. There was no point anymore in denying that she was attracted to the handsome lieutenant. But it could never go anywhere. She had too many trust issues when it came to men. Plus, she doubted he would ever be seriously interested in her—not with his mother's attitude.

Then there was the issue of meeting former jurors. As

much as she begged him to let her come, she really didn't look forward to meeting those who had declared her guilty.

She hoped her face was neutral. "Fine."

"Breakfast will be—"

Shaking his head, Jace pulled a face. "We'll go through a drive-through on the way."

She heard what he didn't voice. No sense pushing his mom any further than necessary. She nodded, then retreated back into her room. His footsteps padded down the hall as he returned to his childhood bedroom. It was probably selfish of her, but she had been relieved when he announced his intention of staying here as long as she was in his mother's house.

She hefted her bags off the bed and stashed them beside the closet. Her suitcase was still packed. She hadn't even opened it. Her sleepwear came from her small overnight bag, which held her nighttime necessities—pj's, toothbrush and paste, and a Bible and journal. Remembering her dilemma over whether or not to bring the small bag earlier, she twisted her lips into a wry smile. Seems she needed it, after all.

An angry shriek woke her up in the morning. She bolted upright in bed, heart pounding. The clock on her nightstand said 5:52. Hurriedly, she arose and dressed in jeans and a checked flannel shirt over a mock turtleneck. Both shirts were faded and hung on her slender frame.

She found Jace and his mother standing in the backyard, Mrs. Tucker making furious gestures toward her house. Mel looked up. She gasped, her hand clutched at her shirt over her heart. Right under the bedroom window where she had slept, in bloodred letters, someone had painted A MURDERER SLEPT HERE.

"That tears it," Mrs. Tucker blazed. "I want her out of my house. Now."

NINE

Silence stretched between them as Jace and Melanie drove. It was an awkward, tense silence. They had left his mother's house within minutes of her declaration. Neither felt like eating, but Jace went through the drive-through at McDonald's, anyway. She was only able to eat half of her breakfast sandwich before her stomach revolted. Queasy, she wrapped it back up. She hated to waste good food, but there was no way she could force any more down.

"You done with that?"

Mel jerked her head up at Jace's terse question. He pointed to the half-eaten sandwich in her hand. She held it toward him.

"Yeah, I can't eat any more. Do you want it?"

He grabbed it out of her hand. She bit her cheeks to keep a smile tucked away.

"I'll take it. I'm starved." He swallowed the sandwich in two bites, then washed it down with coffee.

"Better?" she inquired innocently.

For the first time that morning, he flashed her a smile. "Much. Thanks. We seem to have issues in the morning."

And that, she thought, was all the discussion they were going to have about his mother. Fine with her.

"I'm dropping you off at the hospital for about an hour,

two at the most," Jace stated as he turned smoothly into the parking lot. Mel raised an eyebrow. She hadn't been aware of their plans. "I need to go check in with Paul, update him on the situation. That sort of thing. I've arranged for Sergeant Olsen to stay with you at the hospital."

Sergeant Miles Olsen turned out to be the policeman who had shown up the day she was released. He was a young kid who had just become a cop a year ago. Miles was bright, eager and looked as though he should be wearing a Boy Scout uniform instead of a police one. His shaggy blond hair kept falling across his forehead, and his smile was wide and engaging.

"Don't worry, Miss Swanson," he enthused when he met up with them in the hospital. "I'll keep a real close guard on you. Lieutenant Tucker is depending on me."

"I'm sure you'll be fine," she murmured, her mind on other things.

As they approached Aunt Sarah's room, she heard Seth calling her name. Sighing, she waited for him to catch up. Seth hurried to stand before her, then directed a pointed glance at Miles. When Miles refused to acknowledge him, Melanie intervened…somewhat reluctantly. She wasn't above wanting to see Seth squirm a little.

"Miles, could you let Seth and me have a word, please?"

The young sergeant shook his head, his mouth grim. The expression was alarming. All at once, he truly looked like a police officer. His eyes hardened as they glared back at Seth. Whoa. The hostility leaking from him was nearly tangible. But why? Judging from the confusion marring Seth's normally confident face, he had no clue, either.

"No, ma'am. Lieutenant Tucker is counting on me. I can't let you go off with anyone."

Mel sighed. "Look, we'll be right here. Just step back a few feet so we can talk privately. Please?"

Obviously unhappy about it, but without any real reason to argue, Miles retreated a few feet. His eyes remained
on Seth, though. Seth pointedly ignored him. He reached
out to grab Melanie's left hand, but she moved away. His
hand dropped.

"Mel," he started, then paused, obviously unsure of
how to begin. Melanie decided she didn't feel like waiting for him.

"Why did you abandon me, Seth?" she shot out, accusa-
tion in her voice. "You were my best friend since we were
kids. We always stood by each other. You knew me better than anyone. You knew there was no way I could have
sold those drugs, or that I could have tried to kill myself.
You *knew* that. Yet you didn't even try to fight for me."

Seth hung his head. There was no denying it. And they
both knew it. He had let her down in the most despicable
way possible.

"I'm ashamed of how cowardly I've been. If there was
any chance…"

"Yeah, you acted like you were ashamed. One day we
were in love and engaged, and the next, you were distanc-
ing yourself and treating me like I was beneath you. Even
the other day, you acted like I was—"

Seth held his hands up, nodding his head. "I know, I
know. And I'm sorry. I wish I had done things differently."

"But why did you act that way, Seth? I trusted you."

"My dad put pressure on me to leave you. He felt your
background would hurt his campaign. And it upset my
mom to see him get so upset. She was sick, I didn't feel
I could stand against him." He shrugged. "By the time I
came home, your trial was over and you were already in
jail. "

Melanie realized she wasn't surprised. His father had
always looked down on her. She should have known he

would try to come between her and Seth. What really hurt is that Seth had let him. But Seth wasn't done.

"I suspect he used his connections to speed up your trial so it would be resolved before I came home. The judge and the DA are both golfing buddies. My father has contributed thousands to their campaigns."

Shock tore through her with the force of a bullet, rocking her back on her feet. Sheer grit allowed her to regain her equilibrium even as liquid agony ran raw over wounds she had thought were healed long ago. Whether she had been innocent meant *nothing* to these people. Her future, her *life* were gambled away so powerful men could keep their power. Worse than that, Sylvie had died, and whoever had killed her was still at large, probably preying on others.

"Melly? Are you all right? Mel?"

Disgust boiled inside her, rising and pushing at her until she had no choice but to let it out. Her lip curled and her eyes narrowed. Seth actually retreated a step as she scalded him with a glance.

"You were supposed to love me." The words were bitter on her tongue. "We were planning to vow to forsake all others, remember that, Seth? Good thing we weren't married yet. Because that was an epic fail on your part."

She read his intention to touch her arm and backed away, shaking her head. His hand dropped, desolate.

Miles approached. The look on his face said he would not be gainsaid. "I think it's time for us to continue to your aunt's room, Miss Swanson. Lieutenant Tucker said he would be back within an hour and a half."

Seth sketched a brief salute and departed. She watched him as he strode away, dejection in the slump of his shoulders. She refused to call him back. A whisper in her soul encouraged her to pray for a forgiving heart, but she blocked it out. The shock and betrayal were too new. A throat clearing reminded her Miles was waiting. Setting her jaw, she turned away from Seth and started walking again.

When they arrived at her aunt's room, Miles respectfully waited outside while she visited. She sat by the bed, singing in a soft voice, sometimes praying. Finally, a sense of peace came over her. She forgot about the IVs and the breathing apparatus. Even the monitor's beeping became background noise.

"You ready to go?"

She hadn't heard Jace enter the room, but it felt right that he should be there.

She stood and left with him.

"So, you want to tell me about it?" Jace held open the door for a young woman struggling with an infant car seat. He tipped his head at Mel, nudging her to exit the building ahead of him.

Mel shrugged her shoulders. "Tell you about what?"

Jace snorted. "Please. I can read you better than that. Something has you riled." He cut his eyes at her. "Was it something Seth said?"

"How did you know…? Oh, you talked to Miles, didn't you?" She should have known Miles would feel duty-bound to give Jace a full report. She really couldn't blame the kid for being conscientious.

"Yep. I think the kid has a crush on you. I barely even knew his name before, and now he practically begs to be in on the case. Now spill."

A gusty sigh exploded from her. Jace smirked, amused.

"Okay, okay. Remember when you asked Seth why he hadn't testified? Seth thinks his father made sure that would never happen. His father was concerned that a connection with me would hurt him politically even before Sylvie's death."

"Well, strictly speaking, maybe it could have."

Mel flinched. She was still feeling bruised from her conversation with Seth.

"Anyway," she continued, "the senator convinced Seth to drop me. Then, Seth thinks he might have used his connections with the DA and judge to push the case through, so I'd be locked away before Seth got back."

At least *that* seemed to catch Jace off guard. "Seriously?" he said.

Melanie nodded. "Apparently the senator goes golfing with the DA and judge and has contributed heavily to their campaigns. All that power and influence," she spat out bitterly, "and he decides to use it to keep his son from marrying some bad seed."

"I would have thought, though, that a man like Seth would have made up his own mind. I'm sure he's kicking himself now for being an idiot."

"Yeah, well, he can kick himself all he wants. I'm still not getting back together with him."

Jace stopped. "He wants to get back together with you?"

Warning bells went off in her mind at his stiff tone. Uh-oh. As unbelievable as it might seem, it appeared that Jace was uncomfortable with Seth's renewed interest. Jealousy? She flicked a casual glance his way then bit her lips to keep them from curling up at the corners. A scowl as dark as a thundercloud sat upon his brow. Yep. It sure looked like jealousy to her. It was probably petty of her, but she rather enjoyed the possibility.

It was the last urge she had to smile for hours.

The morning dragged by. The first three jurors they visited all denied receiving any kinds of threats. They also claimed that they still believed Melanie to be guilty. Whether they really believed this or just needed to soothe their consciences was irrelevant. The fourth juror on the list was deceased. He had died after a short battle with cancer over a year ago.

The day wore on. Around lunchtime, they approached a house that was owned by a Maggie Slade, a young woman of about twenty-five. Jace gave her door a brisk knock, but Mel wasn't surprised when no one answered. The newspaper box was overflowing, a pile of rolled-up papers scattered on the porch. The yard had a lonely, neglected feel to it.

"She didn't stop her paper delivery, but her mailbox is empty. My guess is that she took the time to put a hold on that."

"Why wouldn't she stop her paper delivery if she was going away?" Mel queried, although she wasn't sure she wanted the answer.

"Good question. My guess is that she was in a hurry. Maybe panicked. I'll see if I can get a warrant to check this place out. In the meantime, we have more people to visit."

The next two jurors were both males—one older, one about Melanie's age. The old man was adamant that he believed, then and now, that Mel was guilty.

"Where there's smoke, there's fire. That's what I always say." He grunted, then spit a stream of tobacco juice out of the corner of his mouth. Mel sidestepped so it wouldn't hit her shoes. Somehow, she didn't think his atrocious aim was accidental.

The young man didn't seem to care one way or another if Melanie was guilty or innocent. He had gone along with the crowd. "I figured they must know what they were talking about. Besides, the cops can't arrest you if they don't have any evidence. Right?" He looked Melanie up and down. "But you're kinda cute. Hey, now that you're out, ya know, are you free for dinner sometime?"

Jace snorted in disgust. Melanie agreed. Without a word, she went to wait for Jace in the truck.

The next juror, an older woman, patted Mel's cheek and told her she had always wondered if she had been innocent. When Jace inquired what made her vote guilty, the woman looked sad and ashamed.

"I was weak. The others were adamant that I was wrong to doubt the evidence. I gave in. For that I apologize."

"I accept your apology. And I don't hold it against you." Mel kissed her cheek. Then they moved on. Next they learned that another juror, a young man named Steven Scott, had been killed in a car accident about two months ago. They both were feeling fatigued by that time. By three o'clock, they had seen seven jurors. That was when Paul called them into the department. He had had the last juror from their list flown in.

As soon as they entered the room, Mel knew that this was the woman that Alayna had told her aunt about—the other juror who admitted to being threatened. Her movements, her expressions, all spoke of extreme anxiety. When she turned and faced Melanie, her face turned ashen. She cried out and sank weakly in her chair. Melanie felt sorry for her. She was young and pretty. She looked like she should be out having fun, dating and dreaming of babies. Instead, she was here, terrified.

"You know, don't you?" she sobbed.

Paul made the introductions. "This is Miss Emily Keith. May I see you in the hall, Lieutenant Tucker?" Jace nodded and followed him out. Melanie left the room behind him. She wanted to know what was going on, so until told otherwise, she would stick like glue to Jace. Paul barely looked at her when she closed the door behind her. "She's the final juror, I understand?"

"Yes, sir. Except for the one who's missing. I'm still

waiting for a warrant to go search her property." Jace turned his steady blue eyes on the distraught woman sitting in the interview room. "From what she has already said, I think we can assume she was the one who was threatened."

"Be careful with this one. The US marshals are standing by to escort her to a safe house. Hopefully, we'll be able to find whoever is behind this. Then she will be needed to testify. Until then, she and her family will need to be protected."

"Understood, sir." Jace put his hand on the door. "Mel, you need to remain out here for this one."

The urge to argue was nearly overwhelming, but Mel fought it and held her tongue. It would be selfish to allow her feelings to interfere with the investigation. Jace had already allowed her to participate more than he should have. She had to trust him now.

Easier said than done. She bit back a protest as he walked through the door. Patting her shoulder in understanding, Paul accompanied Jace into the room. Folding her arms, anchoring her cold hands in the warmth of her underarms, she rocked slightly back and forth as she stepped up to the window. And watched as Jace disappeared, and Lieutenant Tucker approached the table—a formidable ally, and an equally daunting opponent.

Jace could feel Melanie's stare boring into his back as he marched with authority to the table. He forced himself to focus 100 percent on the shaking woman before him and not think of the woman who was depending upon him to clear her name and quite possibly save her life.

"Miss Keith, another juror came forward and revealed that she had been threatened to cast a guilty vote. New evidence has been found that suggests that Miss Swanson was not guilty. Can you help us? Were you threatened, as well?"

Emily leaped from her chair.

"My family! They threatened to hurt my parents!"

Paul interjected, his voice commanding. "They? Do you have any idea who they might have been?"

"No! Please! My mom and dad. And my kid brother!" Emily grabbed on to Paul's arms, shaking him in her desperation. Paul calmly patted her hand, then removed himself from her grasp.

"No one is going to hurt your family, Miss Keith. They were all removed from their home by US marshals this morning. Even as we speak, they are in a safe location. They will be protected, and so will you, for as long as necessary."

Emily, relieved of her fear for her family, answered their questions, her voice wavering every now and then. When the first threat had arrived in a letter, she had tried to resist it. She had listened at the trial and had even argued with a couple of jurors about what she had felt were inconsistencies in the case. When she had arrived home that evening, her beloved dog was lying dead on her doorstep. A letter was left that stated clearly that her own family would be next if she didn't comply. She folded. And the next day, she had meekly gone along with the other jurors.

Jace and Paul took turns questioning her, rephrasing the same questions, searching for clues, any hint to the identity of the person behind the threats. Finally satisfied that they had everything, Paul rose and went to the door, motioning to a tall man in a dark suit. The quintessential US marshal.

There was something else, though. As she got ready to leave, Emily gasped, her hand flying to her mouth. "How could I have forgotten?"

"What?" Jace and Paul said together.

"There was a man on the jury...Steve Scott."

"Yes, we know. He was killed in a car accident two months ago," Jace informed her. He wasn't trying to be cold, he was just getting impatient.

"Oh, no! I wondered why he had stopped emailing. We dated a few times after the trial."

Jace was slightly amused by that. Only slightly.

Paul and Jace both motioned for Emily to continue. She blushed.

"About six months ago, Steve started hinting that he felt bad about the trial. I had been trying to forget about it, it was such a horrible experience. Anyway, one night...oh, about four months ago, we were talking on the phone, and I broke down and told him about the threats. He admitted that he had received a threat, too."

That got their attention.

"Why didn't you say that in the first place?"

Emily cringed from the anger in Jace's voice. Her voice was wobbly when she spoke again. "He said he didn't feel bad about going along with it because he thought she was guilty, anyways. The threat didn't change his mind. At the time. But later he started to have second thoughts. Felt like he needed to go to the police."

"Well?" Paul demanded. "Did he? Did he go to the police?"

Emily lifted her hands. "I don't know. That was the last time I talked to him. I texted him about a month ago, and I guess I thought he was busy or no longer interested. It never occurred to me that something bad had happened to him."

The woman dissolved into sobs. The marshal escorted her out to take her to her family. Paul flipped a switch so that anyone outside the room would not be able to hear their conversation.

"I didn't have a chance to tell you this earlier. I did some checking on that juror you couldn't find, Maggie Slade. Well, I think she is probably dead. She made an appointment to talk with a lieutenant. She wouldn't say what she wanted to talk about, just that it was about the trial."

"Let me guess," Jace picked up the conversation. "She never showed, did she?"

"You got it."

"Who was she supposed to see?"

"Dan Willis." Paul pursed his lips and raised his brows. "I think that's mighty interesting, don't you?"

Jace laughed. The sound was hollow. He threw his own bomb. "Melanie told me her ex approached her this morning. Said he thinks his old man pulled some strings to get the judge to rush through the trial before he came home from Europe. Old political buddies, or something like that."

Paul whistled. "Man, this case just keeps getting more involved. The judge will be out of town until tomorrow afternoon. Means you won't have a warrant for the juror's house until then. Tomorrow I want you to go to Pittsburgh. See if you can't nose around and find out anything more about what happened to Steven Scott."

"Yes, sir. I'll start at their police department…see what they have. I have my doubts that his car accident was truly an accident. Too coincidental."

"I agree. Today, though, you need some downtime." Paul held up one hand when Jace started to protest. "This is not open for debate, Lieutenant Tucker. Miss Swanson is about done in. She has held her own, but these past couple of days have been extremely stressful."

Well, he couldn't argue with that. The more he considered it, the more he realized that Paul was right. The last thing he wanted was for Mel to collapse on him. Not that she would. That girl might appear frail, but he was beginning to understand that she had some steel in her soul.

They left the police station in silence. The day was unseasonably warm. Mel leaned her head back against the headrest and closed her eyes.

"Hey, are you awake?"

She opened one eye and gave Jace a sleepy smile. "Sort of."

Maneuvering the truck onto the interstate, Jace headed north toward Erie. He clicked the radio on low, and they listened as the sounds of Beethoven filled the cab.

"Where are we going?" she asked.

Jace threw her a smile that barely lifted his lips. She was adorable, her voice sleepy and kind of husky. She had a large red mark on her forehead from sleeping against the window. "I need to stretch my legs. Why don't we head to the mall and just walk around inside?"

"Won't we be kinda out in the open there?"

He could hear the worry in her voice.

"No one knows that we're going. And there are tons of people there. Security cameras. It's not like we're going to be walking along a secluded trail. I have my gun and the chief's orders."

She tilted her head and scrunched up her cute little nose. Why had he never noticed she had freckles? He could see her weighing the idea in her mind, so he threw in an extra incentive. "I'll buy you ice cream."

Her eyes lit up like a Christmas tree.

"I haven't had ice cream in four years. Yes, let's go."

They spent the next hour at the mall. Jace hid a smile as Mel ate her chocolate chip cookie dough ice cream. She ended up with a dot of ice cream on her nose. He pointed it out to her, and she wiped it off. He was almost sorry. She had reminded him of a kid.

Unfortunately, they eventually needed to leave to find her a hotel room. As he unlocked the truck's passenger door for her, she glanced around, her face regretful. He knew the feeling. For a short time, they were able to be two people enjoying a spring afternoon. Now, all the events of the past few days were rushing back, as well as all the reasons he needed to keep his distance from her. It was harder than it should be. She stepped up to the truck, brushing close to him as he opened the door for her. The urge to kiss her overwhelmed him. *Remember Ellie. Don't get too close.*

Jace realized that Mel was waiting for him to shut the door, her forehead scrunched as she watched him. Shutting the door with a shrug, he jogged around to his side of the truck. Within minutes, they were zipping up I-79. Whistling, he kept a constant vigil on his mirrors as he maneuvered through the light traffic. His eyebrows drew together and he stopped whistling midsong.

"The car behind us is too close," Jace observed. He tried tapping his brakes to warn the driver off. No effect. "I didn't think it would be that easy."

"What do you mean?" Mel questioned.

"I mean that whoever is behind us is driving too close on purpose."

Experimentally, he maneuvered into the left lane and sped up. The car behind him followed suit. He pushed the pedal down even more and passed three cars, before pulling behind a semi. Sure enough, the SUV pulled in behind him.

Mel swiveled her head and looked out the back window. "Whoa. Jace, that guy is wearing a ski mask. Who wears ski masks in spring? Creepy."

"Mel, grab my phone and hit two. That's the police station. Tell 'em we require backup."

Mel snatched the phone made the call. The operator dispatched a unit to intercept them.

"Are you able to see the license plate number?" the operator asked.

Mel shook her head, then realized the woman couldn't see her. "No. We can only see the front of the car."

Without warning, the driver swerved to the left lane. Jace hoped he was moving away. That thought disappeared when he whipped out a gun and pointed it toward them. Mel screamed when the first shot rang out. Jace evaded the bullet, but whoever was behind the wheel was a skilled driver. Added to the fact that the little sedan he was driving was faster and more maneuverable than Jace's beat-up pickup truck.

"Hang on!" Jace yelled. He shifted gears and attempted to escape, weaving back and forth so as not to give the shooter an easy target. But he kept up with them. Another shot rang out, and the truck started to go out of control. A bullet must have hit a back wheel. Another shot, and the windshield shattered. A third shot hit the front driver's side wheel, and the truck spun out. It careered off the road and landed in a ditch. The other car slowed as if it would stop, then sped up and raced away.

Jace lifted his head from the steering wheel with a groan. He was going to need to see a doctor. He was pretty sure he had a concussion. He slowly turned his head toward the passenger seat. Mel was leaning against the passenger door, clearly in pain. But alert. Gratitude filled his heart when he saw that she was mostly all right, just a little roughed up. His eyes sharpened on her right shoulder. Her shirt had torn, and her skin was bleeding. Probably from the glass that lay around her. But he could still see that the skin that should have been smooth was puckered in an angry-looking scar.

"Mel," he said, his voice deceptively soft. "What happened to your shoulder, honey?"

Mel looked down in confusion. When she saws the exposed scar, she grimaced. "It's an old injury. It happened when I was a kid. Nothing to worry about."

Jace disagreed. He had been in the police force long enough to have seen a variety of wounds and the scars they leave, and he knew that was a stab wound.

TEN

It was almost an hour before Melanie was able to stop shaking. The memory of that man in the ski mask as he casually aimed a gun at them was sure to haunt her dreams for a long time.

The backup unit arrived to pick them up and bring them back to the station. Jace had filed his reports and they gave their statements. Now they were on their way out the door. Jace's truck was out of commission, so they got into his cruiser.

He sighed. When she raised her eyebrows, he shook his head slightly.

"I miss my truck." Men.

Soon they were on their way. On their way where? Well, that was a question Jace had yet to answer.

He apparently had something else on his mind. She soon knew what.

"So, the stab wound? Wanna tell me about that?"

She wanted to shrug it off as nothing, but the stubborn set of his jaw told her that wasn't going to work. She sighed. Brushed her hair back from her face with an impatient gesture. She was stalling, and she knew it. When she cut her eyes in his direction, his raised eyebrow told her that he knew it, as well.

"Fine. When I was ten, my father got roaring drunk. I had set the table for dinner and had given him a knife that hadn't come completely clean in the dishwasher. He got angry with me."

Jace looked appalled. "So he stabbed you? Didn't you go to the hospital?"

"Yeah, and he told them some tale about me being klutzy while handling the knife. He was such a charmer, such a well-known figure in the community, they never questioned him." She tried to ignore the pity warring with disbelief on his face. "Anyway, not long after that he and my mom died, and I went to live with Aunt Sarah."

Da da DUM. A tri-tone bell-like noise issued from the console area. Mel glanced at it. Irene's name flashed on the display. Saved by the bell, she thought, more than ready to end this conversation. Jace pushed a button to put the call on speaker.

"Yeah, 'Rene. What's up?"

"Hey, buddy. You can bring Melanie back to Mom's house tonight." Irene's voice, sounding distinctly smug, answered him.

"Umm, Irene," Mel interjected, "I don't think that's a good idea. Did you see the back of your mom's house? She was pretty steamed."

"Yes, of course I saw that. I heard about it, too. And she was angry. But then I overheard about you getting shot at over the police radio."

"How?" Mel started to ask. Jace broke into the conversation.

"Irene's husband is a cop, too. You haven't met him yet because he's away at a training seminar. Irene, how did you convince Mom?"

Irene sighed. "It wasn't easy. But you know how she hates bullying. When it was clear Melanie is a target, she decided to give her another chance. Not to mention that Paul had someone come out to the house to install some state-of-the-art security system, on the police department's dime, I might add. Official police business, he said."

Air whooshed out of Melanie's lungs, accompanied by a distinct wheeze.

"Where's your inhaler?" Jace immediately asked.

She fished around in her pocket and pulled it out and used it.

Within minutes Jace had changed course and was heading back toward his mother's house. It was with trepidation that Melanie stepped from the vehicle, unsure of what kind of welcome awaited her. Did Mrs. Tucker blame her for putting Jace in harm's way? Or had Irene somehow managed to convince her mother that Melanie wasn't the evil temptress she had been made out to be?

It was evening now—the sun had set an hour ago. A rumble from her stomach reminded Mel that they had yet to eat dinner.

She heaved herself from the car and felt as if she had concrete blocks tied to her feet as she walked beside Jace up to the house. She blinked as lights flooded the yard. Ah. The new security system. She tensed as Mrs. Tucker opened the inside door and waited for them. Once inside the house, Melanie stiffened her shoulders, knowing she had to meet the other woman's accusing eyes eventually.

She lifted her head.

And got a shock.

Instead of the hostile glare she had received only that morning, Jace's mother watched her with eyes filled with pity. Pity? Why would Mrs. Tucker pity her now?

Dread curdled in the pit of her stomach. She tamped down the urge to flee, to hide. Whatever had happened to make Mrs. Tucker look at her that way, she didn't want to know. Because whatever it was, it would probably devastate her.

She was right.

"Melanie," Mrs. Tucker said in the gentlest voice Mel had ever heard from her. It was a voice reserved for frightened children and wounded animals. "Melanie, one of the officers watching your aunt at the hospital called twenty minutes ago. I'm sorry. Your aunt is gone."

"Gone?" Mel repeated, her mind numb. "Gone," she said again, tonelessly. Why were her ears ringing?

"Mel, maybe you should sit down." Jace's voice was far away.

It was the final straw. Mel's mind had reached its limit. She swayed, feeling her ears buzz as she passed out.

Mel was sitting on the window seat in her room the next morning when someone knocked on her door. She was tempted to ignore it, let whoever was on the other side think she was sleeping, but she couldn't abide even that small deception. Besides, she had a feeling Jace at least might be concerned about her. After she had revived from her faint last night, she had allowed Irene to assist her as she got ready for bed. She had slept dreamlessly for almost twelve hours. Without turning her head now, she called out, "Come in."

Irene walked over, a light breeze of perfume coming with her. She didn't say a word. Just leaned over and gave Melanie a hug. Then she sat down on the window seat beside her. Melanie allowed a few minutes to pass in companionable silence before she faced Irene. Jace's sister was watching her with compassion. But not pity. Mel was thankful for that. Pity was a hard emotion to deal with.

"I'm okay," she assured Irene. "I'm even peaceful. Aunt

Sarah is in Heaven, and she has perfect knowledge now. She knows the truth."

Irene tilted her head, reminding Mel of a delicate bird. "That's good. I'm glad for you on that score. Still, it has to be difficult for you. You never even got a chance to be together again before all this happened."

Feeling her throat tighten with emotion, Mel nodded.

"My mom had Jace make breakfast. Will you come down?"

"Jace cooked breakfast?" Melanie was entranced by the idea of him providing for his family in such a way. She wished she could have seen him as the teenager he had described to her, the one who stepped up to take care of his family after losing his father. Was he ever in trouble, or was he always determined to be a cop? She would ask him someday.

Irene scoffed at her question. "Of course he cooked breakfast. I wasn't here, and my mom is dangerous in the kitchen. If she had made breakfast, it would have been peanut butter toast. Not that she doesn't try. She does. She just can't seem to get the knack of it. I can't think of a single recipe she has made successfully."

Melanie trailed along beside Irene, laughing softly. Jace turned at the sound, a relieved look on his face. She realized he'd been worried about her. Even Mrs. Tucker gave her a strained smile. That smile coming from a woman who had treated her with hostility recently almost undid her.

"He never even went to work this morning," Irene muttered next to her ear. "He was so concerned. He called the office and requested permission to work from here. I think he was planning on waiting here all day until you came down."

Melanie flashed the woman a warning look. The last thing she wanted to do was make jokes at Jace's expense.

Not after all he had done for her. She pushed away the thought that there might be another reason she didn't want to make fun of him. Irene wasn't impressed. She smirked, then sauntered around to her chair.

Jace strode toward her and placed his hands on her shoulders, squeezing them gently. His gaze searched her face as if trying to gauge her mental state.

"You hanging in there?" he queried, his voice pitched low so only she could hear.

Tears spurted to her eyes. Her throat ached as she held them back. Unable to speak around her grief, she answered him with a stiff nod.

Jace gave her one last squeeze, then gently shoved her toward a chair. She sat, not even giving him token resistance. She was far too spent for that. Her world had been tipped on its edge again, and she felt it was all she could do just to hang on. It was sheer reflex to hold the warm coffee mug Jace placed before her between her chilled palms. She inhaled the pungent aroma. Jace made coffee the way she liked it, strong. She sipped the bitter brew and felt herself settle. Jace set a plate with an omelet filled with veggies in front of her. Not in the mood to eat, she pushed her food around on the plate, only vaguely aware of the conversation around her. It wasn't until Irene and Mrs. Tucker finished eating and excused themselves that she spoke.

"I want to talk with that doctor from the hospital. The one we talked with last time. Dr. Ramirez, I think his name was." The words popped out of her mouth. She grimaced. "Sorry. I didn't mean to be so abrupt."

"No, that's okay. I was thinking the same thing." Jace sipped his own coffee, his eyes deep in thought. "We can go right after you eat."

"Oh, but I'm not really that hungry…"

Jace stopped her with a look.

"I know you don't feel like eating, Mel. Could you try? Maybe just a bite or two? Today's gonna be a hard day. You'll need your strength."

Melanie scowled, but obliged him by taking a small bite of the spicy omelet. Whoa. It was delicious. Once she started eating, her appetite kicked in. She stared at her plate in dismay minutes later. She had wolfed down her breakfast with as much gusto as a teenage boy. Jace chuckled and tossed her a smug wink. Her stomach fluttered.

Mel was suddenly conscious of how much she had come to rely on him. How had she let her guard slip? He was a good man, but she had seen too many "good" men turn on a dime. Her father let alcohol and drugs change him. Seth let his father's opinion sway him. Well, she wasn't going to give Jace Tucker a chance to break her heart.

At the hospital, Jace leaned against the registration desk and flashed the young woman sitting there a pleasant smile. He could practically feel Mel's eyes shooting daggers at him. His smile threatened to become a grin. He wasn't flirting with the girl, just being polite. Well, okay, maybe he was flirting a little. He was regretting being so tender with Mel that morning. He couldn't let her get the idea that they could ever be anything other than friends. He didn't want to hurt her any more than she was already hurting. As soon as this case was closed, he needed to walk away from her. The thought should have brought him relief. Instead, it made his heart ache.

"Y-yes?" the brown-haired girl behind the desk stammered, her eyes wide. "May I help you?"

"I hope so—" his eyes flashed to her name tag "—Diana. I need to locate Dr. Ramirez. Is he in today?"

The girl cocked her head. Her eyes lost their starstruck look and became puzzled. "No-o," she responded slowly.

Jace exchanged a glance with Mel.

"Do you expect him in later today?" Mel butted in to the conversation.

"I'm sorry, but there is no Dr. Ramirez here."

"Not today?" Jace persisted, although his instinct told him that she meant more than that.

She confirmed it when she shook her head firmly.

"No, I mean not ever. There is no doctor by that name working here."

"Then who was the doctor in charge of Sarah Swanson when Dr. Jensen was gone?" Not bothering to give the flustered receptionist time to respond, Mel whirled on Jace. "That man, the one in Aunt Sarah's room—"

Jace nodded at Mel, than turned back to the girl at the desk. "The room where Sarah Swanson was is now a crime scene. No unauthorized personnel are to enter. Have hospital security posted outside that door until backup arrives. Is that clear?" Jace used the radio on his shoulder to call in a team to do the forensics. Mel looked shell-shocked. He needed to discuss the situation with her, make sure she was coping.

Unwilling to hold this conversation in front of witnesses, Jace placed a firm hand at her elbow and started to steer Mel toward the waiting area. She jerked her arm out of his grasp and walked, stiff-backed, into the room. Jace frowned at the back of her head. The spacious room was empty, the only noise coming from the television set. Jace increased the volume, allowing the soap opera to act as a screen for their own conversation.

"Mel, I am really sorry about this, but we have to assume that your aunt fell prey to another attempt on her life. It would be fair to guess that the missing Dr. Ramirez had a part in that."

"I hate this!" Fists clenched at her side, Melanie's body

shook with frustration. Her jaw tightened, and he thought she was probably grinding her teeth. "I mean, I knew that was probably the case, but hearing you say it, to know such evil is so close—"

"I know, and I hate that I need to be so blunt, so cold about the whole thing, but you need to stay alert. A killer is on the loose. I need to get a team in here. Then I'll get you back to my mother's."

He should have expected resistance, really. Mel lifted her pointed little chin and folded her arms across her chest. The daggers shooting from her eyes told him she needed answers as badly as he did, and she wasn't going to walk away without a fight. She opened her mouth to argue. He held up one hand to forestall her.

"Look, Mel, Paul needs me to go to Pittsburgh to check on the juror who died in a car wreck. You know, talk with the officer in charge of that investigation. I can't do that if you're around. I won't leave you unprotected. You know that."

He waited until a security guard could come in and stay with Mel, then left. He returned to her twenty minutes later. She was subdued.

"Okay, Mel. I ordered a warrant to look at the security disks. The team has arrived and is going over every square inch of your aunt's room for evidence." Not that they'd find much.

"Why don't you sound confident?" Mel asked.

He sighed. He hadn't been as good at hiding his doubts as he'd thought.

"Your aunt died last night. They've already cleaned the room. Since she was in coma already, the doctor on call declared that she died of natural causes so no one thought to take any precautions to preserve the room. The one good thing is that there wasn't a new patient assigned to the room yet. Any way you look at it, though, it's not very likely the team will find any new evidence. So let's hope the security disks will."

They waited for an hour before the warrant arrived. They watched the monitors in silence as various nurses and staff walked past the room. Every now and then the camera caught a nurse entering the room. She'd check vitals and mark the chart. After half an hour, the man they knew as Dr. Ramirez entered the room. He checked the vitals and marked the chart, same as the nurses had. Then he glanced over his shoulders at the door. Keeping his eyes on the door, he slipped a hand inside his coat and pulled out a long needle and attached a vial to it. He moved over to the IV and injected the liquid. Pocketing the vial and needle, he sauntered back to the door and exited. The camera clearly showed him talking for several seconds with the security guard before walking to the elevator. A minute later, the entryway camera caught him, now dressed in jeans and a T-shirt, leaving the building.

"There's our guy," Jace murmured. He rubbed the back of Mel's hand with his thumb. All at once he realized what he was doing and dropped her hand. He casually leaned forward as if needing to see the screen better. He wasn't sure why he wanted to mask his attempt to keep his distance, other than he didn't want to hurt her feelings.

"There's something familiar about that guy. Don't know what. Maybe it'll come to me on the drive."

ELEVEN

Melanie had been none too pleased when Jace informed her that he would be traveling to Pittsburgh alone. Oh, sure, she knew he would accomplish more without her, especially in a police station where everyone would see her as nothing more than a convict. She would have been in the way. In her mind, she understood that. In her heart, though, she was uncomfortable being away from him. Until that moment, she hadn't realized just how safe he made her feel.

She could not fall into that trap again. Yes, she trusted Jace. He was a brave man, a man who took his call to protect and serve seriously. But he was still a man. She needed to put her trust in God. He would care for her. She wouldn't let herself need anyone else.

A sigh left her. She could no longer procrastinate. Jace had contacted Paul that morning before he left. Mel knew that two officers would be with her most of the day. She had reluctantly let Jace convince her to allow Irene to deal with most of the funeral arrangements. Mel was of two minds about that. On the one hand, she was grateful that she didn't need to be out and about by herself on such a gloomy mission. On the other hand, she felt she owed her aunt so much, and now she would never be able to repay her.

Still, she was alive. Her aunt would not approve of her moping around when there were things to be done.

Her steps were sure when she walked into the bright kitchen for lunch. She was pleasantly surprised to see Irene sitting at the table reading the newspaper, a fresh carafe filled with coffee in front of her.

"Hi." Jace's sister greeted her with a warm smile. "Have a cup and I'll tell you our plans for the day."

Melanie raised her eyebrows. "Oh? Do we have plans?" Not very hungry, she popped a bagel into the toaster and poured herself a steaming cup of coffee. She couldn't resist bringing the cup to her face to inhale its rich fragrance. Even if she had hated the taste, she would have still loved the aroma. Good thing she liked coffee.

Irene gave a vigorous nod. "Of course. I figured you probably need to get out of my mother's house. We are going shopping."

"Oh, Irene, that's so sweet. But Jace—"

"But Jace nothing. My dear brother is at his protective best. He told me you were in danger. I understand that. I called the department and got us our own personal body-guard. Some newbie named Miles is coming with us. And another officer will meet us at the mall."

Melanie shook her head, doubt creeping into her eyes. "I don't know, Irene. It seems so silly, going shopping now. My aunt just died, you would be putting yourself at risk…"

Irene stood and swept across the room to Mel. Her expression serious, she placed her hands on Mel's shoulders.

"Melanie, I know this is a trying time for you. I don't mean to make light of the situation. But you can't stop living. You will be in an open public place, and there will be a police car directly behind us at all times and two officers dogging our every step." Mel wavered. It sounded as though all the necessary precautions were in order. Irene hugged her. When she stepped back, her eyes were filled with compassion. "And honey, the shopping trip is not silly. There is sure to be a huge crowd, not to mention media, at your aunt's funeral. You need something to wear that actually fits you."

Okay, that made sense.

"Besides, think of how disappointed Miles will be if we don't go! I fully expect him to have the sirens going the whole way up, he's so excited about being given such an important duty."

Laughing softly, Melanie shook her head. "I almost feel sorry for him. The kid is so new, he squeaks. But he seems sincere."

Satisfied, Irene smiled. "Then it's settled. Go get dressed and we will be on our way to the mall. You are in desperate need of a new wardrobe. Maybe we can get you something fun, too. Like possibly an outfit to make my brother's head swim."

"Irene!"

Irene snorted. "Don't 'Irene' me. I see the way you two look at each other. And I think it's great. It's about time my brother let himself feel something more than duty." Sadness touched her pretty face. "And I hate the way he blames himself for Ellie's death."

"How could that possibly have been his fault?"

"Oh, sweetie, deep inside he feels that he should have been able to protect her—or at least figure out what was wrong in time to get her some help. She was his baby sister, but in many ways he was a father to her after our dad died. He tried to be a father to us both. I was twelve, but Ellie was only eight."

The image of Jace as he was at her trial came to mind. Forbidding, angry and somehow broken. She hadn't understood the turmoil he had felt, but she had sensed it. Now she mourned for his grief.

Mel set her brush down just as Miles pulled into the driveway. Grabbing her purse and coat, she hurried down the stairs so that he wouldn't be kept waiting. He was such a sweet guy. He almost tripped over his own feet in his eagerness to take her arm so she wouldn't slip on the ice. There was nothing kid-like in the way he handled his car, however. He expertly wove in and out of traffic. Even though the traffic in Erie could be heavy, his car was behind theirs every time she looked back. Mel was impressed in spite of herself.

As she and Irene chatted on the drive, she admitted to herself how much she had missed this, having another woman to talk with. The fact that Irene was so willing to overlook her past was a huge blessing. Melanie felt free to talk without fear that she would somehow say something that would make her listener walk away in disgust.

At the mall, she tried to ignore the stares and whispers when someone recognized her, no doubt from the newspaper photos from the day she was released. The first time someone pointed at her, she actually cringed. She sneaked a peek at Irene to see her reaction. Irene acted as if she hadn't noticed a thing, but Mel saw her jaw clench. Expecting Irene to call an early halt to their adventure, she was pleasantly surprised when the other woman proceeded into yet another store, the two officers falling into step behind them. "Come on, let's find you something."

Find something they did. It was a soft black dress that fell in graceful folds to Mel's calves. It was modest and subdued. Perfect for a funeral. What she hadn't expected was the way it made her look. Regal. She looked regal. She lifted her chin and allowed the corners of her mouth to lift. There. A perfect smile. Not happy, not cheeky. But confident enough to help her brave those at the funeral.

"How does it look, girlfriend?" Irene called through the door. "Let me see."

Feeling shy, Mel opened the door. Irene clapped her hands, delight written all over her face.

"Oh, my brother's gonna forget his own name," she gloated.

"Irene, that's not why we're shopping," Mel reminded her knew friend softly.

Irene cast her an ashamed look. "Sorry. Guess that was thoughtless. But—" she slid a sly look at Mel "—I still think you're going to make his eyes cross."

"You don't believe I did it, do you?" The moment the question left her lips Mel wanted to call it back. Irene, however, was already answering.

"I never have. Even during the trial." She saw the question in Mel's eyes. "Jace was too tormented. Too torn. I could tell he was second-guessing himself. And I know he was under pressure to close the case. He thought he was letting Ellie's death distract him from the truth. But Jace doesn't get distracted. His instincts are usually right on."

Melanie threw her arms around her new friend's neck.

"Thank you," she choked.

"You're welcome," Irene whispered back, her own voice cracking. Then she cleared her throat and pushed Mel back, a teasing smile on her pretty face. "Now I want to go try on some shoes. Why don't you go back into the dressing room and change, then come join me."

"Shoes? You bet!"

Back in the changing room, Mel quickly changed out of the elegant dress, determined not to keep Irene waiting.

A gentle knock on the door interrupted her musing.

"Miss?" a soft female voice, sounding very young,

called to her. "Your friend asked me to have you try on this, as well."

Melanie peeked through the door and saw a young girl, probably about fifteen, standing there, popping her bubble gum as she waited. Despite the ring in her eyebrow and the bright pink hair, she was surprisingly innocent-looking. Mel opened the door far enough to take the plastic store bag from her.

"Thanks."

She watched the girl swagger back toward the store entrance, replacing her earbuds as she went. Had she ever been that carefree? Sighing, she returned back into the dressing room. She held on to the bag with one hand while she slid the latch into place, then she opened it and reached down inside, expecting to grab on to fabric. Her mind froze when her hand closed over a thick coiled body with smooth, dry scales.

A bloodcurdling scream escaped as she dropped the bag in terror. Two hissing black snakes emerged, staring at her with baleful eyes, flicking their forked tongues in her direction. She whispered a prayer and tried to unlatch the door with fingers that shook and fumbled. Panic threatened as her sweat-slickened fingers slipped off the latch. She grabbed it again. Finally. But when she tried to open it, the door thudded under her hands. It felt as though something heavy had been thrown against it. She shoved against the door. It wouldn't budge!

She whimpered as she remembered the barricaded door in her bathroom while the kitchen was set on fire. Flattening herself against the wall, she fought to control her breathing. Hysteria was building inside her. Spots danced before her eyes as she struggled to stave off a panic attack. Snakes were her greatest fear.

"Black snakes. They're just black snakes. Not poisonous." She repeated the mantra to herself again and again.

"Mel! Hold on, Mel," Irene called out. Bumps and scrapes could be heard as whatever blocked the door was moved. At last, the dressing room door was wrenched open. Irene stood in the entrance, her face pale. She gasped and shrieked as one of the snakes writhed toward her. Yanking Mel through the opening, she quickly slammed the door closed before the serpent could escape.

"Someone call the manager, and security! We have a situation here."

Jace was ushered into the chief's office at the Pittsburgh precinct. Chief Martha Garraway greeted him with a firm handshake and a welcoming although professional smile.

"Lieutenant Tucker. Please, sit down." She motioned toward a couple of standard-issue chairs across from her. "I hear you have questions regarding the death of Mr. Steven Scott."

"Yes, ma'am." Jace cleared his throat. He needed to step carefully. In no way, shape or form could he even hint that the officers under her command had not done their duty. "A case from my county seems to be linked to his death." He drew a deep breath and said a quick mental prayer for guidance. Chief Garraway nodded for him to continue.

"Four years ago, a young college student was sold some tainted drugs and died as a result. An anonymous tip led us to a Miss Melanie Swanson. I myself collected the evidence against her. It seemed a simple open-and-shut case. Miss Swanson herself appeared to OD, a suicide attempt complete with a note wherein she confessed to selling the drugs. The level of drugs in her system caused some memory loss of the night in question. She pled not guilty, but was convicted of manslaughter and served her time in prison." He refused to allow himself to dwell on those four years. She had forgiven him and claimed he had saved her. He had to move on.

"A few days ago she was released. Since that time, her life has been repeatedly threatened and her aunt has died in suspicious circumstances. Two jurors have admitted to being threatened into finding her guilty during her trial. One of those jurors has been murdered. The other said that Mr. Scott had also been targeted and that he was coming to talk with your detectives before he was killed. My chief has put me in charge of locating Mel—er, Miss Swanson's attacker." Of all the stupid— Did he really just refer to her as Mel in front of the chief? What was he, a rookie?

Chief Garraway arched a brow at him. "Apparently you know Miss Swanson pretty well."

"Yes, ma'am. Well enough to have proof that she was set up." No way was he adding any more than that. Let her think what she wanted.

Garraway narrowed her eyes, considering. She decided. Folding her hands in front of her on the desk, she gave him what he wanted. "Mr. Scott came here. He spoke to one of our finest detectives. When he was killed the next day, my officer immediately suspected foul play. He ran a thorough investigation and discovered that Mr. Scott's vehicle had been tampered with. It was no accident. We are still working to apprehend the one responsible. At the moment, however, we have no suspects. My detective has gone undercover to try to locate the perp."

"Would it be possible for me to review the case files, Chief?"

Chief Garraway was way ahead of him. "I thought you might want to. When your chief contacted me, I had the files brought up and copied for you. I took the precaution of removing my detective's name from the reports. I know you will understand my wish to keep his identity private."

"Absolutely, Chief."

Chief Garraway led Jace to an empty conference room and left. He spent the next hour poring over the files. Steven Scott's story matched Emily Keith's. His car had been expertly sabotaged. Whoever had taken him out, the guy was a pro. He returned the file to Chief Garraway, thanking her for her time and cooperation.

"I believe, Chief Garraway, that when you find your perp, we will find ours, too. I would suggest keeping the communication open between our departments."

"Agreed." Garraway stood and extended her hand. "I look forward to working with you, Lieutenant Tucker."

Satisfied, Jace left. He sat in his car long enough to shoot an email to Paul, then he started his engine. *I wonder what Mel did today?* he thought to himself. He smiled as he imagined her impatience at being kept in the house with only his mother for company. They would probably avoid each other. He was nearing the parking lot exit when his phone chirped. He had an email. He glanced at the phone and saw it was from Paul. *I'd better look at this before I go.* A minute later, his satisfaction with the day's work had dissipated. Aghast, he stared at the email on his phone. He read it over twice. He could see Irene wanting to take Mel shopping. But Paul? He shook his head in disgust.

"I can't believe this," he muttered. "He really let those girls go shopping?"

Urgent now, he tossed his phone down on the passenger seat and pulled out into traffic. It would be at least ninety minutes before he could get to the mall.

WHAM!

The car lurched forward as it was struck from behind. Jace just avoided slamming into the guardrail. He jerked the cruiser back just in time to see the car shift into the lane beside him and speed up. He could make out broad shoulders, but the driver's face was hidden behind a scarf and a baseball cap pulled low over his features. Remembering being shot at before, Jace risked a glance in the rearview mirror. No one was behind him. His lips a grim line, he slammed a foot down on the brakes and held tight to the steering wheel. Unprepared, the other car shot past him. Jace sped up and flipped on his siren. He caught sight of the license plate and radioed it in.

"That plate belongs to a vehicle reported stolen last week."

Of course it does.

Jace continued to follow the other vehicle. The driver accelerated and swerved onto an exit ramp. Jace maneuvered onto the ramp, then lost the other car when a convoy of tractor trailers came between them.

He banged his hand on the steering wheel. He had been so close to catching this guy. At least he knew that he was being followed this time, which meant that Mel should be safe for the time being. He furrowed his brow. Something gnawed at him. Grabbing a piece of spearmint gum from his pocket, he chewed as he mulled over the events.

There was quite a difference between shooting at people and leaving threatening pictures. Even the mannequin and the rock incidents were only threats. And then there was the fire. That was more than a threat. So was the attempt to shoot at them while they were driving.

His mind latched on to the idea that had been brewing inside for the past couple days.

There had to be more than one attacker. Nothing else made sense. Now if he could only prove his theory.

The dispatcher came over the radio, reporting an incident at the mall. He held his breath, knowing there was no way he could get there to make sure Mel was safe.

"Officers on the scene. No injuries reported."

Jace let out the breath he was holding on a prayer of thanksgiving. Mel was in God's hands. He had to trust. Although that did not mean he couldn't use his siren.

Flipping his siren back on, he moved into the right lane to pass the slowing traffic.

Hold on, Mel. I'm coming.

TWELVE

Melanie sipped the Coke the store manager had brought her. The officer who had responded to the call closed his notebook as he finished his notes. Irene hovered like a mother hen, alternating flapping her hands and wringing them. Mel was touched by her concern, and bit her tongue to keep from asking Irene to please sit down.

"The pet store on the lower level reported they sold two black snakes to a kid about an hour ago," the officer informed her. "Since you appear to have been targeted, I would guess she was paid to do it."

Melanie remembered the young girl who had handed her the bag.. Before she could ask about her, Irene's cell phone rang. The manager and the officer both frowned at the redheaded woman, making her flush.

Irene grabbed the offending phone and took it outside to answer it.

"Hey, Mom. There's been a problem—" Mel heard before the door shut behind Irene. Great. One more thing Mrs. Tucker could blame her for, just when she thought she'd been making progress.

One person looked more miserable than she felt. Miles stood off to the side, his face pale. He held his hat in his hands, wringing it mercilessly. It would probably never look the same again. He had apologized to her at least a dozen times. If he tried again, she just might start pulling out her hair. She didn't see how he could have possibly stopped the incident. It's not as though he could have come into the dressing room with her.

Irene returned. "Sorry. I turned the phone off."

The officer frowned at her, jerking his head to motion her all the way inside. She hurried back to Melanie's side.

"Madam, I'm so sorry that such a thing happened in my store." The manager stood before Mel, his wide forehead slick and sweaty. "Please, allow me to make amends. What were you purchasing this afternoon?"

"I was buying a dress and shoes for my aunt's funeral." She indicated the dress and shoes sitting beside her. Irene had still been holding them when they had been escorted to the back of the store.

His face grew another shade paler.

"Please, the dress is on the house. Accept it with our apologies." He made a funny little bow as he spoke.

"Sam, do you know who this is?" a young clerk, no more than sixteen, interrupted. "I saw her on the news. She's the chick that killed that college kid. I think she probably killed her aunt, too."

Melanie gasped as she took in the girl's smirk. Irene rounded on the girl like a mother tigress.

"How dare you! Is this the way you treat customers in this store? She was nowhere near her aunt when she passed away. What a horrible rumor to spread." Unfortunately, Irene could not say she hadn't killed Sylvie, Mel thought, her lips twisting. She may believe Mel was innocent, but the law still held that Mel was guilty.

The horrified manager shushed the girl and sent her to work on inventory in the back room.

Red-faced, he apologized again. "Take the shoes, too."

* * *

Irene plopped down on the living room couch and set her feet, ankles crossed, on the coffee table. A stack of magazines fell off the other side. Mel moved to pick them up, but Irene motioned her away. She pointed a stern manicured finger at Melanie.

"You. Sit," she ordered. "You deserve to relax after a day like today. I nearly passed out when I saw that snake crawling around in that room with you."

"*You* nearly passed out? How do you think I felt when I reached into the bag and actually felt the snake? I hate snakes with a passion. I can't believe I was dumb enough not to question someone handing me a bag. I should have looked inside it, not just reached in with my bare hand." The memory of the dry, slithery coils had goose bumps breaking out on her arms. She shuddered.

"I couldn't believe that horrible girl. To say such a thing to a complete stranger!" Irene huffed.

Mel smiled at her new friend. "I was shocked, but you know she only said what others were thinking." Irene started to protest. "Stop, Irene. You know I'm right. I think Jace believes I was set up because of the events in the past few days. You believe me because of Jace. But can you honestly say that if it weren't for your brother, you'd think I was innocent?"

"Of course I would!" Irene protested weakly. Her eyes caught Mel's before she flushed and looked down at her lap.

Melanie sighed, disappointed. Which was unreasonable, she knew. If everyone thought she was guilty, how could she expect a different response from Irene?

"But, Melanie, that doesn't matter!" Irene exclaimed. "I do believe you! Wondering whether or not I would have in different circumstances is pointless."

Melanie shoved her bitterness aside. "You're right, of course."

Irene gave her a relieved smile.

The front door slammed.

"Mel? Irene?"

Jace. Her heart sped up.

"In the living room," Irene hollered.

Brisk footsteps pounded toward them. Jace stopped just inside the room, his gaze fused with Mel's. For a moment, they just stared at each other. Irene's chuckle broke through to Mel, and she dropped her eyes, feeling heat spread up her neck and into her face.

"I heard on the radio that there was an incident at the mall today. Please tell me you weren't there."

Flustered, Mel exchanged a glance with Irene. Mel couldn't lie, though. Especially not to Jace. So she nodded. His eyes fixed on her in frustrated disbelief and he raked his hand through his hair. She rushed to explain.

"We had two officers with us, and Paul knew where we were going."

"But why did you need to go? Particularly now?"

Mel stood and went to Jace. She put a hand on his arm, feeling the muscles jump beneath his shirt. He looked... what? Disappointed? She couldn't bear to think she had let him down.

Before she could say anything, Irene rushed in to defend their excursion.

"Honestly, Jace, we had to go! Melanie had no clothes that were appropriate for her aunt's funeral. And you know people will be watching. Please don't be mad." Irene gave an exaggerated pleading look.

Jace rolled his eyes. "I will never understand women and their clothes. All I heard on the radio was that there was an incident. Fill me in, will you?"

Choosing her words with care, Mel told him what had happened, then waited. She wasn't sure what she expected. Anger, maybe. Or frustration. Maybe even a lecture.

What she didn't expect was gleam in his eyes.

Finally, a break in the case.

"Mel, first of all, are you all right?"

She nodded. "I'm fine. It shook me up, but I'm okay."

"Good. I think you'd better sit down."

She bit her lip and looked up at him anxiously. He had the urge to lean down and kiss her sweet lips. Not that he would, of course, because that would end any chance he had of protecting his battered heart from her. Instead, he focused on the matter at hand.

"Let me tell you what I found out today." He told them about his conversation with Chief Garraway.

"I believe that Steven Scott was killed because he told someone he was planning to go to the cops. I don't think the killer knew he had already gone."

"You weren't able to talk with the detective who had spoken with him?" Irene asked her brother.

"Couldn't. He's undercover, trying to find the person who sabotaged Scott's car. She wouldn't even give me his name. It would jeopardize his cover."

He then related the events that occurred on his drive home. Both women gasped, their hands over their mouths, concern darkening their eyes. It warmed him to see the caring on their faces.

"It was a stolen car. I suspect the car that was used when we were shot at was stolen, too."

"So you're no closer to catching this guy?" Dismay colored Mel's voice.

"Ladies, one good thing has come of this." He laughed at their matching skeptical expressions. "I'm serious. I have been confused by the way this perp had no patterns. It struck me that maybe there were two perps, not one."

"Two!" Mel jumped to her feet.

Jace came to his feet as well. He reached over and gathered her hands in his. "Mel, think of it. That's the only explanation that makes sense. How could someone corner you at a store and go after me at the same time? There have to be two different perps. My question now is whether they are working together or separately."

Mel squeezed his fingers so hard, he wondered if she was cutting off the circulation. He doubted she was even aware of what she was doing.

"What's your gut instinct tell you?" she asked him.

"My gut says they are two people with separate agendas. That's why the one is intent on frightening you into leaving town. A bully, so to speak. The other one, though, is out for blood."

"I'm so sorry, Jace."

Jace was astonished to see the tears pooling in her eyes.

"Good grief, Melanie, why are you sorry? You've done nothing to deserve this." He smoothed her hair back from her face.

She caught his hand in her free one. "Jace, the only reason you are in danger is because of me."

He scoffed. "I would have become involved sooner or later. My conscience, if nothing else, would have driven me to act."

"He's right, Mel." Irene stepped up beside Mel and placed an arm around her shoulders. Jace was touched to see the affection blossoming between the two women. "Whoever these guys are, they're playing a sick game. They need to be stopped."

"And Mel—" Jace placed his knuckle under Mel's chin to bring her face back to face him "—you don't deserve this." The desire to kiss those lips was pulling at him. It was becoming harder to remember why he was resolved not to fall for her. But he had to. Especially now. Because her life depended on his ability to do his duty, and he couldn't do that if he let emotions cloud his thinking. With an effort, he stepped away from her and moved to the window.

Irene chuckled.

"Where's Mom?" he asked his sister, mostly to distract her.

Irene adopted an indifferent expression and shrugged her slim shoulders. "I don't know. She wasn't here when we got home."

"She called you while we were at the store," Melanie tilted her head.

"Yeah, but she just said she was running errands."

"Well, before she gets home, let's go over what happened this afternoon again." Jace gathered up paper and pencils and made a list of the events and their approximate times.

"See?" He pointed to an item on his list. "You were in the dressing room at two. I was in my car at two forty-five. It's a good two hours from Erie to Pittsburgh. There's no way—"

"Hey, kids, I'm home!"

Jace and Irene both rolled their eyes. "In here, Mom."

The click of heels hitting the linoleum flooring echoed in the kitchen. They waited patiently for Mrs. Tucker to reach the living room. She took in the sight of the three people in the living room, her eyes lingering on Mel. For a moment, Jace worried that he might need to intervene between the two women again. Then, in the oddest turn of events, his mother grew flustered and patted her hair, a sure sign she was feeling uncomfortable.

"Melanie." Her voice sounded strained, nervous.

"Mrs. Tucker?"

"Mom, are you okay?" Jace was starting to get just a little tense. Was she getting ready to try to kick Mel out again? He couldn't force his mother to accept Mel into her house, but he was running out options.

"I'm fine, dear." Mrs. Tucker fixed her troubled gaze on her daughter. "Irene, would you mind giving us a moment? I would like to talk with Melanie alone."

Irene looked surprised, but she kissed her family farewell and headed toward the front door. "Not a problem. I have to get home, anyway. Tony has a meeting tonight, so I need to get home in time to get him and the boys' dinner."

"Give them a hug from their favorite uncle." Jace adored the rambunctious one- and three-year-old boys.

"Only uncle," Irene snorted as she shrugged into her coat and departed, leaving the scent of her perfume in the air.

Jace was slightly concerned. His mother had not been Mel's biggest fan. He folded his arms across his chest and waited. Mel would not be facing this conversation alone. He loved his mom, but he knew she could be a real harridan when the moment warranted it. He wasn't exactly sure what he expected her to do.

Nothing could have prepared him for what happened next.

Mrs. Tucker walked over to Melanie and took one of her hands in her own wrinkled one. Mel rocked slightly, almost like a deer preparing to flee. "Melanie, I need to ask for your forgiveness."

"Wh-what?"

"Mom?"

She turned her sorrowful eyes on her son. "I have been thinking all day of what happened yesterday—how someone shot at you and Jace. And then when I called Irene, she told me about the incident at the mall. I don't know if you are guilty of the crime you went to jail for. Jace and Irene don't seem to think so. But regardless of your guilt or innocence, I know that in trying to force you from my home, I placed you and Jace in danger. I know my son well enough to know that he will protect you with his life if necessary. I only have two children left. I would never have forgiven myself if anything had happened to him because of me." She looked down. "And I know he would suffer if anything happened to you on his watch. I can't let him go through that again." Tears filled the woman's eyes.

Mel reached out her free hand and placed it over their joined hands. "Of course I forgive you, Mrs. Tucker. You were not at fault."

His chest ached with tenderness for this woman.

He was in trouble. Epic trouble.

Mel felt as if she had been hit by truck. The sight of Mrs. Tucker begging for her forgiveness was surreal, to say the least. Only yesterday, this same woman had regarded her with open hostility. Even Jace appeared to be stunned by the change.

A few minutes later, Mrs. Tucker left to head upstairs to take a brief nap before supper. Jace muttered something about being thrown for a loop. Mel nodded, distracted. Yes, she knew that feeling well. It seemed something was always throwing her off balance lately. She frowned at Jace. He was the biggest offender, she realized.

"Mel," Jace's voice called her back to the situation at hand. "I need to talk with Paul. We need to plan for security at your aunt's funeral."

"You really expect trouble at a funeral?" Mel was horrified that anyone would consider using such a painful event for violence.

His face compassionate, Jace nodded. "I wish I could say no, but yeah, I expect trouble. What kind of trouble, I'm not sure. I hate to sound cold, but we need to be prepared for anything."

"What about the calling hours? Will we still have those?" It was common practice in this part of Pennsylvania to have calling hours the day before the funeral. One afternoon session and one evening one.

Jace considered the question, then shook his head. "No. I'm sorry, Mel, but there are too many variables. Our police force is going to be stretched pretty thin with the funeral. I think the calling hours would be more than we could safely handle. You really don't want to be in the public's eye that much, anyway, do you?"

The mere idea filled her with dread. "No, but it would be for Aunt Sarah, not me. I could do it for her."

"I know you could, but I don't think it would be a good idea. Let me call Paul, and we'll see what he says."

Paul agreed with Jace. There would be no calling hours. Only a funeral at the church and a graveside service. Paul was all for ditching the procession to the cemetery, but Mel was stubborn. Her aunt deserved it. She had been a kind and faithful servant of the Lord her whole life. Mel was sure there were many friends who would need to grieve and say their final goodbyes to her. She was determined to let them have that opportunity.

Paul finally stopped trying to change her mind. "All right, Melanie. We will allow the graveside ceremony to happen. But you need to promise to follow my instructions to the letter. Because your life might depend on it."

THIRTEEN

As Mel got ready for bed that night, she thought about the strategy Paul and Jace had developed for the funeral. She grimaced. The one person she did not want to see there was Dan Willis. It made sense, though. At the cemetery, she would be out in the open, exposed. As Jace had pointed out, the more officers on scene, the safer she would be. She just wished Lieutenant Willis didn't intimidate her so much. Jace will be there, she reminded herself. She trusted him to keep her safe.

She went to bed that night with all the events and details of the day whirling in her mind. How on earth she would ever get to sleep when she was so wired was beyond her. Exhaustion got the best of her, though. She drifted to sleep almost as soon as her head hit the pillow.

The casket was being carried down the aisle of the church. She walked behind it, dressed in black. The organ was playing, but it was out of tune, the sound warped.

Suddenly, the church erupted in whispers. She whipped her head frantically from side to side, staring at the people in the pews, who were pointing their fingers at her, murmuring. What were they saying? She couldn't make out the words. It felt as if her ears were filled with cotton.

All at once, the pallbearers stopped. Jace turned away, disgust etched on his handsome face. "You! Murderer!"

Then the murmuring grew louder, clearer. "Murderer! Murderer!"

She clapped her hands over her ears, but strong hands grabbed them and pulled them away. She tried to free herself, looking over her shoulder to see her captor. Officer Dan Willis was holding her, a leer on his face.

"Melly," Seth sang out, appearing before her. "It's time to take your medicine!" He held out his closed fist. Slowly, oh, so slowly, he opened his fingers to reveal a handful of large pills. Officer Willis held her as Seth stepped closer to her, an evil grin stretching his mouth. He grabbed her chin to force the pills into her mouth.

"Jace, help me! Help me!"

But Jace pivoted, abandoning her as he walked from the church.

Mel bolted upright in bed, the sound of her pounding heart loud in her ears. Her T-shirt was soaked with sweat, and her hair was melded to her skull. Her breath wheezed in and out as she reached over to the night table and fumbled for her inhaler. Trembling hands lifted the canister to her lips, and depressed it.

Once her lungs were able to fully expand again, she walked to the window and peered out. The full moon glowed down on the yard below. Restlessness shivered in her bones. She needed to move. She walked on bare feet to the door and peered out into the hall. Careful to make no sound, she made her way to the kitchen and poured herself a glass of milk. The light came on, startling a gasp from her. Whirling, the milk splashed on her wrist.

A rumpled-looking Jace, complete with five-o'clock shadow, stood blinking in the door.

"Mel? You okay?" His voice was husky with sleep.

She opened her mouth, but found it was too dry to speak. She took a swig of milk. "Fine," she croaked.

He walked closer and his hand snaked out and caught her elbow. He gently pulled her under the light. Warm blue eyes scrutinized her face. She imagined it was probably pale and wan from both her nightmare and lack of sleep. She swallowed when he tenderly brushed her hair back from her face. Her breathing felt constricted again, but this time it had nothing to do with her asthma.

"You don't look fine, Melanie. Trouble sleeping?" he murmured.

She nodded, not trusting her voice.

"You want to tell me about it?"

She shook her head. Then immediately contradicted herself when she admitted, "Bad dream."

"Oh, Mel. C'mere." Jace enfolded her in his arms, resting his chin on the top of her head.

She allowed herself to sag against him for a few perfect moments before stiffening her spine. Drawing away from him, she forced a smile to her face.

"I'm okay," she insisted. "Just too much going through my mind."

He waited.

"What happens if we can't pick out the guy from the hospital?" she voiced her fear.

"If we can't pick him out of the book, then we will work with a police artist to get a likeness that we can circulate. It's amazing how fast we can identify people with technology. It's very possible that we'll find his likeness in the national database."

Mel bit her lip, considering this. Satisfied, she nodded.

"What else was bothering you?"

"How do you do that?" she exclaimed.

"What?" he asked, a smile playing around his mouth.

"How do you know what I'm thinking about?"

Jace placed a gentle finger in the center of her forehead.

"Your forehead creases when you are worried." He followed the furrow with his finger. "I figured there must be something else bothering you other than ID'ing Ramirez, because the crease stayed."

"I'm worried about the funeral."

"I'll do everything in my power to protect you. You know that." His head tilted.

She hesitated. "I know you will. But I can't help thinking about the mob scene the day I was released. I feel like I'm going to be on parade, with lots of judgmental stares turned my way."

Jace opened his mouth to answer, but she never knew what he was going to say. The security lights in the yard flared on. A loud clang sounded right outside. They leaped apart, startled. Jace dashed to the window, Mel right behind him. They laughed softly when they saw a large raccoon scurry from the tipped-over garbage can. Jace placed an arm around Mel's shoulders and squeezed.

The phone on the wall rang. Jace answered, keeping one arm firmly encircling Mel's shoulders. "Hello? Yes, the security lights went on. It was a raccoon. Thanks for checking."

He hung up the phone. Mel realized his arm was still around her shoulders and stepped away. She deliberately crossed the kitchen to put some distance between them. Jace gave her a funny look but didn't remark on her actions.

"That was the police station. The security system alert went off. Guess we can safely say it works," he joked.

Something was off. His face had changed. Some of the softness she had seen mere moments before had disappeared. It was disconcerting how quickly his mood changed. Fearful of what he might be thinking, she decided she had better make her exit.

"Guess so. Well, I'm off to bed again. See you tomorrow."

Without looking back, she escaped to her room. She needed to get a handle on this. Jace had made it perfectly clear that the last thing he wanted was a relationship. Was he regretting hugging her? Even though he had hugged her to offer comfort, it had felt like more. She had to protect her heart. She needed to be sensible. She hoped that in the morning she would be able to act as though nothing had occurred.

And speaking of sensible…she would be worthless if she did not get some sleep. Determined, she got into bed and pulled the snuggly comforter up to her shoulders. This time sleep evaded her.

She pondered Jace's certainty that something would happen at Aunt Sarah's funeral. Irene had stated that her brother's instincts were usually on target. Mel couldn't help but fear that the worst was yet to come.

The next morning, she awoke, feeling nervous. She took her time showering and getting dressed in her jeans and a white turtleneck with a jade-green knit sweater over it. As she brushed her hair, she briefly toyed with the idea of wearing a little makeup. Snap out of it, Mel, she chided herself. This is a serious situation.

Finally ready, she walked down to the kitchen. Jace had made pancakes. There was something to be said for a man who could cook, she decided, biting into the fluffy pancakes. She licked a small dot of syrup from her fingers, then looked up to find Jace's eyes riveted on her.

"What?" she asked, defensive.

He grinned. "You look like a little kid. I can't believe what a messy eater you are."

She grinned back. Her smile faded as the electricity crackled between them. The memory of the hug last night lingered between them. Abruptly, Mel jerked her gaze from his. She gathered up her dishes and started clearing the table. Jace helped her, but neither spoke.

It might be a very long day, she thought as they made their way to the car in silence.

Jace held the door open for Mel and allowed her to precede him into the police station. As she passed him, he inhaled the scent of her freshly washed hair. Weary from lack of sleep, he was revitalized by the smell.

Unfortunately, there was a new awkwardness between them. He knew that hug in the kitchen was the cause. Did she regret it? He could tell that her walls were back up. A twinge of regret hit him, even though he knew it was a good thing. They had no future. He couldn't afford a romantic entanglement. His job depended on it. He reminded himself that romance and duty didn't mix. Couldn't. Yet he found himself wondering what would happen if he took her out. After the case was closed, of course.

Shaking his head to clear it of these thoughts, he led the way to Paul's office. The door was open, and Paul was sitting inside. Unexpectedly, so was Dan Willis. His spine stiffened. Jace instinctively stepped in front of Mel, shielding her with his body. No way was he letting Dan get near her again.

Neither Paul nor Dan appeared concerned. What was going on?

Paul motioned them into the room. "Close the door behind you. I don't want to be overheard."

Jace put his hand on the small of Mel's back, feeling the tension in her. He slid his hand up to her shoulder and squeezed. He hoped she got the message that he was here.

He would stay by her side. Dropping his hand, he turned and closed the door, making sure he heard the *click* of the latch before he turned back.

Once they were all seated, Paul started.

"Jace, Mel, I need to let you in on what's been going on. I know that Chief Garraway told you she had an officer undercover." He gestured to Dan. Jace's jaw dropped.

"You! You were the officer investigating Steven Scott's death?"

Dan cleared his throat and scratched the back of his neck. "Yeah. Steve came to see me several months back. He told me how he and at least one, possibly two, other jurors had been threatened. I told him I'd look into it. Before I'd even finished reading about the case, he was dead. I found it suspicious, to say the least. When I investigated the wreck, I found that his car had been sabotaged. When I talked to my chief, she in turn called Chief Kennedy, and they agreed to bring me here temporarily to work undercover."

"Chief?" Jace addressed his friend, struggling with this new information. "I assume you didn't inform me to make sure there was no risk of a leak." He knew his tone was a little cold, but he couldn't help feeling angry. Paul had known him forever. They had been hanging out at each other's houses since they were kids. Jace still considered Paul his closest friend. Paul knew he could trust him.

"Please believe me, Jace, I would have informed you if I could have. But there were lives at stake. Knowing that Miss Swanson was being released soon made it even more important that Dan be able to continue his investigation. I did everything I could to protect her. I had her release time changed at the last instant. I had you act as her bodyguard. Still, a mob amassed outside the courthouse. How did they know her release time? And Sarah Swanson and Alayna Brown were both attacked." He glanced at Melanie. "I will always regret that we couldn't protect your aunt, Miss Swanson. She was a fine woman. One of best I've ever known."

Jace could see Mel's lips tremble. She bit her bottom lip and nodded. He put his hand over the one clutching the armrest of her chair. Paul raised one eyebrow, but didn't say anything.

"If you were trying to protect me, why did you treat me so horribly?" Mel questioned Dan. Jace was pleased to note that her voice, though husky, was strong. He was so proud of her.

"Sorry about that, ma'am." Dan apologized in a sincere voice. "I thought it would look more genuine if I acted as if I believed you were guilty. I probably could have toned it down when it was just the two of us, but I figured it would look more natural if I could get you to really dislike me. Then no one would suspect I was actually working to help you."

The lieutenant then looked Jace in the eye. "I'm sorry, sir, for appearing so belligerent. With Miss Swanson's release date leaked, the chief and I worried about someone here not being completely trustworthy."

"That's why we didn't tell you, Jace." Jace swung his head to stare at Paul, shocked. Did Paul think he might have leaked the information? Paul held up his hands and shook his head. "I know what you're thinking, Jace. The answer is no, I never thought you were the leak. You're the most honest man I know. I couldn't take the chance of someone listening in."

"But then why are you telling me now?" Jace narrowed his eyes, glancing between the two men.

Paul rubbed his hands over his face, suddenly looking tired. "You seem to have become a target, too. With

Mrs. Swanson's funeral looming, I need to have you on the same team."

Okay. That answered most of his questions. Except one.

"Why," he growled at Dan, "did you leave Mel alone at her house?"

Dan flushed. "I knew you'd eventually ask that. Chief Garraway called me and needed me to check on a lead. I honestly did call the sergeant on duty to cover for me. He was literally two minutes away from the house. I know I should have waited for him to arrive, but I figured Miss Swanson wouldn't be unguarded for more than a minute. It was an error in judgment on my part."

As much as he wanted to remain angry, Jace knew holding a grudge wouldn't help them get whoever was terrorizing Mel.

"Let's focus on seeing if we can find this dude who was impersonating a doctor," he suggested.

For the next hour, he and Mel pored over the books of known criminals. When he flipped the last page, Mel sighed, her face discouraged.

"Hey, it's okay." He patted her shoulder. "I really didn't expect to find him so easily. Honest. We'll just go up to the second floor and meet with the artist. She'll help us get a good likeness, then Paul will circulate it. I think we'll have better luck with that."

Within another hour they had a sketch of "Dr. Ramirez" drawn. Mel drew in a sharp breath beside him when the artist showed them the final sketch. He could relate. It was an uncanny how she captured the features of a complete stranger just on their descriptions.

The artist stood. "I'll just get this to Chief Kennedy so he can get it to the other precincts."

"I'm starving. What about you?" Jace stood, then held out a hand to help Mel to her feet.

"Not starving, but I could eat."

"Let's go to the Amish restaurant across the street," Jace suggested. "They have the best chicken and dumplings."

Before long, they were sitting down to a hearty meal. Feeling some of the tension dissipate, Jace reflected that they were probably free to enjoy a quiet meal.

"I can't believe you brought her here."

Or not.

Jace looked up, resigned. Senator Travis and his wife approached their table. The senator had his usual sneer on his face. Mrs. Travis showed no emotion whatsoever. She did appear to be a little thinner than the last time he'd seen her, and her color was off. He remembered that she was ill. Lagging behind his parents was Seth, tugging at his collar and appearing uncomfortable.

Jace kept his face carefully controlled. He managed to look at Mel out of the corner of his eyes. Her face was blank, although her fingers plucked nervously at her napkin.

"Senator, Mrs. Travis. Travis." Jace greeted their visitors.

"Lieutenant Tucker, if you keep hauling that woman along with you, people might start getting the wrong idea. You best start minding your reputation." The senator's booming voice hushed the conversations around them.

"Sir, I think you might want to be careful what you say," Jace warned.

"Dad, let's go," Seth muttered, his glance straying to Melanie before he looked away.

"You were smart to break off with this woman when you did, Seth. She's trouble." Senator Travis curled his lip and narrowed his eyes. "Haven't you noticed that people around her seem to get hurt? I'd be careful if I were you, Lieutenant."

Senator Travis smirked—a sly, unpleasant expression—as Jace surged to his feet, furious.

"Easy, son. I'm just stating a fact. I don't think we've seen the end of the troubles caused by this woman."

He led his family away. Seth threw an apologetic glance over his shoulder, but Jace ignored him—as did Melanie, he noticed. He sat down and swiftly sent a text to Paul. It seemed he had a new suspect for his list.

They paid their bill and walked across the street to the car. Jace unlocked the doors. His phone chirped. Glancing at the text, he said to Mel, "Paul wants us to see him for a minute before we head back to my mom's house. Let's go back into the station to see what he wants."

Jogging around the car, he put a hand on Mel's elbow and steered her back toward the station. They were almost to the door when he pulled her to a halt.

"Oh, wait. We should lock the doors." He held the car remote toward the vehicle and clicked twice to lock it. The horn gave a slight beep. They turned to resume walking. The blast as the car exploded into flames sent them both flying forward.

FOURTEEN

"Oof!" Jace hit the ground with a thud and grunted as the wind was knocked from him. Mel hit the ground five feet away from him and lay still where she landed.

"Mel!" Frantic, he ignored his own aches and pains as he jumped up and ran over to her. Pounding footsteps had him grabbing his service revolver and whipping around to face whoever was coming at them.

It was Seth. A Seth very anxious about his ex, judging from the wild look on his face.

"I called 911! An ambulance and the bomb squad are on their way." Seth skidded to a halt beside Jace. "Has she moved?"

"No. You'd better take a look at her."

Seth gave him a wary look. "Could you put your gun away, do you think?"

Jace muttered under his breath as he holstered the weapon. He hadn't realized it was still in his hands.

The men knelt on either side of Mel, who was stirring. The police station doors slammed open as Paul, Dan and half a dozen other officers and workers came running out of the building.

"Jace! What happened? Are you two all right?" Paul

shouted, his calm mask slipping as he sprinted toward his best friend.

Mel picked that moment to moan. All attention shifted to her as she opened her eyes. At first her face was confused; her gaze seemed unfocused. Within seconds, though, her expression changed. Her eyes widened and the fear crossed her face. Until she locked glances with Jace. His heart thudded as her gaze calmed. Emotion clogged his throat.

He had come so close to losing her.

He couldn't understand how she had become so important to him so fast. He had been determined not to get involved with anyone. What was he going to do now? He was no prize for any woman, not with his baggage.

The ambulance siren distracted him.

Within minutes, he and Mel had been corralled by the medics and were getting their vitals checked. Neither had suffered any serious injuries. A few scratches, and Mel had a nasty bump on the back of her head. It wasn't a concussion, though. He had been concerned about that when the bump was discovered. So was Seth, he guessed, watching the other man's intense concentration as the on-duty medics checked her out.

By the time they were declared fit, the bomb squad was on the scene, poring over the destroyed cruiser.

"Sir! We have something here," a junior bomb squad member yelled to his leader.

"I'll be right back," Jace told Mel. "Dan, stay with her."

"Yes, sir." Jace nodded in approval as Dan took up his position next to Mel. He frowned when Seth sat next to her on the other side. Mel looked a little too comfortable chatting with her former fiancé. He gave Seth a stern stare, which the other man ignored. There was nothing he could do. The sooner he found out what the bomb squad had found, the better.

Jace hurried over to the huddle of officers and the bomb squad team. A small piece of debris sat in the palm of the leader's hand.

"What exactly are we looking at, Trevor?" Paul inquired.

"This here, boys and girls, is what is left of a do-it-yourself car bomb. Whoever built this little baby knew what they were doing. See this wire?" he pointed to a small wire, barely discernible from where Jace was standing. "I suspect that this was connected in such a way that when you unlocked your car door via the remote control, it would go into ready mode. As soon as the car locked again, which it would have done automatically once you started driving, it would activate the detonator."

"When was it put there?" Jace asked. "Is there any way to know?"

"Well, when is the last time you used your remote to unlock the door?"

Jace thought back. "Yesterday afternoon. I was in Pittsburgh." He generally didn't bother to lock his car doors at home. No one did. It was a bad habit, but he was grateful for it now, as it had literally saved his and Mel's lives.

"Okay, well, then I would estimate it was set sometime in the last twenty hours or so." He slipped the remains of the bomb into a bag held out to him, then removed his gloves. "One more thing. Whoever set this bomb was no amateur. This was a professional."

"What? You mean a hit man?" Jace exclaimed. He and Paul both turned to look at Melanie. She was still sitting between Seth and Dan, laughing and shaking her head at something Seth was saying. At that moment, she looked completely young and innocent. It was hard to believe a hit man was after her. Because Jace was fairly certain he was only collateral damage. Whoever had set that bomb wanted Mel out of the picture.

Whatever doubts he still clung to about Mel's innocence melted away. Someone, maybe even a couple of someones, was trying too hard to silence her. Someone who was afraid her memory might resurface.

Paul fell into step beside him. They started to walk back toward Mel and her impromptu guardians.

"I need to get into Maggie Slade's house." Jace kept his voice low so as not to be overheard. "I have a hunch that we'll find a clue of some sort there."

Paul, too, kept his voice pitched low. "I'll call the judge as soon as I return to the office. Let him know the case is getting out of hand and we need immediate access."

"Appreciate that," Jace murmured, never taking his eyes from Mel's beautiful face. The sun came out from behind the clouds, and she tilted her face up to the warm rays, closing her eyes. His chest tightened. He found himself actually rubbing his hand over his chest, it ached so badly.

"Jace? You okay?"

Jace looked at Paul in surprise. For a moment, he had forgotten that he wasn't alone.

No. He wasn't alone. Even when danger was near, God was with him. He needed to entrust Mel's care to God. Ask Him to help him keep her safe. Mentally, he turned the task over to God. Resolution entered his soul. And peace.

"Yeah, I'm good," he replied, steel in his voice.

The day of the funeral dawned cold and clear. Frost coated the grass and the windshields of the vehicles. The sky was a brilliant blue, the sun shining bright and blinding. It looked as though it should be warm, but when people walked outside, their breath misted in front of them.

Jace waited in the living room for Mel and his mother to join him. He repeatedly tugged at his necktie. It seemed way too tight. Jace hated the constricting feeling at his throat. He had dusted off his best suit for the occasion. It hadn't been worn since Ellie's funeral. Good thing it still fit. It had never even occurred to him until that morning that he should have checked before.

He took out his phone and checked the time. They should have left two minutes ago. What was taking those women so long? As if on cue he heard the click of heels and the swishing of skirts in the hallway. His mother entered the room first, looking elegant in her black dress and pearls. But his attention did not remain on her for long. Mel entered the room, and his throat closed.

Today, she wasn't Mel. No, today she looked like a Melanie. Feminine and poised. She held her head high, though he could see the fear behind her eyes. Even in mourning, she took his breath away. That's when he knew. He was lost. He walked over to her and bent down to kiss her cheek. Standing so close to her, he could hear her breath hitch. He held out his arm to her.

"You'll be fine, Melanie. I'll be with you. Even when I'm acting as pallbearer, someone will be with you at all times."

"I know," she whispered, her voice faint. He was glad to note that it was steady.

"Got your inhaler?"

She nodded once. "In my purse."

"All right, then." He turned and offered his other arm to his mother. "Irene called," he said. "She's already at the church. Let's motor."

Fifteen minutes later, they pulled up in front of the church. As expected, the place was packed. Sarah Swanson had been a beloved member of the community for al-

most sixty years. There was not a person they met who
didn't have a story to share. Yet there were others, those
who stood back and watched with cold, narrowed eyes.
How many of those had come for a show, to see Mel and
either mock her grief or accuse? Instinctively, he pulled
his arm closer to his body, bringing her a step nearer. He
would protect her.

Irene greeted them with a serene expression. She
hugged her mother and brother before embracing Mel and
placing a kiss on her cheek. She turned her head and whispered in Melanie's ear. Jace couldn't make out the words,
but he caught Melanie's sniffle and her small nod. He left
the women with Dan and Miles. Paul arrived and took his
place behind them. Jace approved wholeheartedly. Mel was
surrounded by those who would keep her safe. Then Seth
arrived and squeezed in beside Paul. Paul greeted Seth
politely, then turned his curious eyes on Jace.

What could he say? The man could sit wherever he
pleased. Besides, the more the merrier if it kept Mel safe.
It could be worse. He could be sitting beside her.

Jace went to the back of the church and took his place
as a pallbearer. The ceremony itself went off without a
hitch. The news cameras had not invaded the sanctity of
the church, which he was thankful for. He even had a moment where he let himself hope that this day wasn't going
to be the circus they had feared.

He should have known it wouldn't be that easy.

The media were in place at the grave site before the
mourners even arrived. As the hearse led the parade of
cars with purple funeral flags into the cemetery, Jace felt
Mel shiver beside him at the sight of the cameras and reporters. It resembled the day she had been released from
prison. He looped an arm around her shoulders.

At the grave site, he exited the car first, then held out

his hand to help first his mother, and then Mel, from the car. A zealous reporter hurtled toward them, his microphone held out in front like he was preparing to pass along the baton at a relay.

"Melanie!" he barked at her. "What do—"

Mrs. Tucker stepped in front of Mel and held out her hand like a traffic cop.

"Young man, this is a funeral, not a carnival. Have respect for the dead," she reprimanded the reporter. Jace ducked his head, hiding a smile. He recognized his mother's teaching voice.

"This might be a funeral, but that girl is nothing but trouble." Jace clenched his jaw as the protestor he recognized from the courthouse stepped forward. "My niece would still be alive today if not for her." He pointed one meaty finger at Mel, who paled.

"Sir," Jace ground out, "I am truly sorry for your loss. Your niece deserved better. But Melanie Swanson was not responsible for her death."

A startled murmur swept through the onlookers. Miles's eyes widened and Dan whistled. Jace grimaced. He flashed an apologetic shrug at Paul. He hadn't meant to let the cat out of the bag so prematurely, but Mel deserved to be able to lay her aunt to rest in peace, free from undeserved accusations.

"What are you saying? Has she managed to deceive the police, too?" the uncle demanded in a near shout.

"No, sir. New evidence has surfaced that, we believe, will prove her innocence."

The uncle looked skeptical. "If she isn't responsible, than who is?"

"We are investigating, sir. We will let you know when we can."

The funeral continued, but Jace could tell there would be questions afterward.

He was wrong, though. As soon as the graveside service ended, Paul orchestrated a police escort back to the car. When Jace made to enter the car, though, Paul pulled him back.

"I'm sending Miles and Dan with Melanie." He fished a paper out of his jacket. "Here's your search warrant. I want you to go to Maggie's house now and search it before the press gets wind of what you're doing. Because once they know, the killer will know."

Mel was quiet the entire ride back to the church. She knew it was customary for the funeral committee at the church to put together a lunch at the social hall, but her stomach quailed at the idea of trying to eat right now. She was aware of Miles and Dan holding a hushed conversation, but she tuned them out. All she wanted was a bit of breathing space.

She had almost fallen over when Mrs. Tucker scolded that reporter as if he were a disruptive student in her classroom. And then Jace had stepped up and defended her, in front of all those mourners. In front of the TV cameras. She had seen Paul's expression. He had not been pleased. Of course, whoever had it in for her would now know that the police suspected Sylvie's killer was still on the loose.

Where was Jace, anyway? He had handed her into the car, then taken off. Dan and Miles had slid into the car with her instead. She liked Miles well enough, although he didn't instill confidence the way Jace did. Dan, though, still intimidated her a little. Oh, she knew he was one of the good guys. He had explained his behavior, and she believed him. It was just a little difficult to reconcile the polite police officer she had seen in Paul's office with the sneering lieutenant sitting in front of her.

No, she didn't feel as safe with these two as she did with Jace. Where was he? She knew it had to be something urgent that had taken him away. His face went all intense as he talked with Paul. He practically ran to get into Paul's cruiser with him. She leaned her head against the cold window, idly watching the scenery fade as her breath fogged up the pane. She continued to muse on Jace's quick exit until she felt a hand on her arm. She rotated her face toward Mrs. Tucker so that her head still lay against the glass. The coldness felt soothing to her.

"Melanie," Mrs. Tucker said, "we've arrived at the church."

Eyes widening, Mel leaned forward to peer out the front window. They had indeed arrived. She had been so focused on her thoughts, she hadn't even noticed that the vehicle had stopped.

Inside the building, people were milling around chatting. The aromas of a variety of hot dishes mingled in the air. No one outright glared at her, but she couldn't help but wonder if people were whispering about her. Bundled in her coat, she started to feel uncomfortably warm. She didn't want to remove it, though. It gave her an added layer of protection. It was ridiculous, she knew, to feel naked without her coat on, but it was like a security blanket.

She couldn't stay in this building. She couldn't. Where could she go? She just needed a place to hide for a few moments. Suddenly it dawned on her. Of course! Everyone expected her to be here. If she ducked out quietly and went to her Aunt Sarah's, who would suspect anything?

It would be stupid to just leave unprotected, though. She looked around. Miles. He would take her. And Dan?

No. She knew he was trying to help, but she didn't trust him. She pulled Irene aside.

"I need to leave for a few minutes. I'm going to ask Miles to take me to my aunt's house. Would you tell people I just needed a moment or something? Please?"

Irene stared at her. "Are you kidding me? Do you know what my brother would say to me if I let you go off on your own, even with Miles with you? No way, my friend. I'm coming, too."

Mel started to argue, but Irene thrust out her jaw in a manner so like Jace's, she weakened and gave in. "Fine. But we need to convince Miles."

Miles needed lots of convincing. Only after thinking through the whole plan to verify that their escape would, in fact, be completely secret did he agree. Irene left to grab her coat quietly. When she returned, the three managed to escape to his car. Within minutes, they were speeding toward her aunt's house.

Mel couldn't believe how much she had missed this place. Even though it felt empty without her aunt, it was filled with memories. Her chest loosened and she could breathe again.

They had taken three steps from the vehicle when the first shot rang out. It slammed into the driver's side door, mere inches from where they had stood moments ago.

Irene screamed and grabbed on to Mel. With a strength she didn't know she possessed, Mel yanked the taller girl behind the cruiser and forced her down into a crouch. Miles was right behind them. He pointed his gun at the trees where the shots rang from and fired. A strangled yelp came from the woods. Then one more shot. Miles ducked, but Mel watched in horror as a blood stain blossomed on his shirt. He lifted his gun and shot once more. Crash.

Something fell. Seconds later, they heard feet pounding in the opposite direction. Miles slumped to the ground.

Mel grabbed the radio from his shirt and pushed the button on the side the way she had seen Jace do.

"Help! Can you hear me?" she screamed into the radio.

"Identify yourself. You are on a police station," the dispatcher replied.

"Please, I'm with Sergeant Miles…Miles. Oh, no. I can't remember his last name. Please He's been shot. We need an ambulance."

The dispatcher sprang into action at the news that there was an officer down. An ambulance was dispatched at once.

Miles roused a few minutes later. His breathing was labored and his face was ashen, but determination shone on his face as he struggled to talk.

"Melanie," he gasped. "I'm sor…sorry. I never meant to hurt you. Never meant… Must believe me." Irene gasped beside her.

"Hurt me? Miles, what are you saying."

"The rock. Phone calls. Pictures. Even the snakes. All me."

This had to be a horrible nightmare. Soon she'd wake up and find she's imagined it all. She knew it wasn't, though. Miles was bleeding next to her, and even now she could hear the ambulance siren.

"What about the mannequin?"

"Me."

"The shootings? The fire? The car bomb?" Jace had sworn there was another villain, but she wanted to make sure. "Aunt Sarah?"

"No, I didn't do any of that. I only wanted you to leave. Never tried to hurt you."

She believed him. But she had to understand. "But

Miles, why?" Her throat ached and her eyes burned, but she refused to break down now. She needed more information.

"Sylvie…my stepsister. Dad married her mom. She was four…I was six. They divorced when I was sixteen. I kept in touch with…stepmom. When Sylvie died, her mom— her heart broke. She cried…when you got out. I couldn't stand her pain."

"Her uncle didn't recognize you."

"He hadn't seen me…ten years. My stepmom and he had a…falling-out. I was a kid." His eyes fluttered closed. He looked as though he were forcing himself to continue. "Sylvie had a half brother." His voice faded. Just before his eyes closed completely, he said, "Seth…Travis."

The paramedics came and loaded Miles in the ambulance. Dan arrived, looking both furious and frantic. He didn't say anything as he motioned for the women to get into his cruiser.

Mel and Irene just looked at each other. Mel wondered if her expression was as shell-shocked as Irene's. Miles's confession had completely floored her. Her emotions swung back and forth like a pendulum. She was furious with Miles for putting her through such grief. The thought of the mannequin hanging by the back door or the snakes in the dressing room still made her break out in a cold sweat. She could imagine, however, his agony in watching his stepmother cry for her lost daughter.

Then his last words hit her. She grabbed Irene's arms. "Did he say that Seth Travis was Sylvie's half brother? My ex-fiancé was related to the girl I supposedly killed?"

Irene stared back at her, her eyes huge.

"That's what he said, which means…"

"Senator Travis was Sylvie's father!" Mel finished for her. "What I want to know is, did he know it?"

FIFTEEN

Jace sat beside Paul on the way to Maggie Slade's house, drumming his fingers impatiently against the dashboard. Paul had the speakerphone on so they could both listen to Dan as he related the morning's events.

"Where are Melanie and Irene now?" Jace demanded. He couldn't believe the trouble those two had gotten themselves into. All they had to do was remain in the church social hall until they could be escorted home. Was that really too much to ask?

"Irene's husband came and picked her up. He was pretty upset. Melanie is here beside me. She's glaring at me. I think she's miffed that I'm not letting her explain things in her own way."

"Well, that's just too bad. Put her on." There were shuffling noises as Dan passed the phone to Mel.

"Jace?"

"What were you thinking, Mel! Any of you could have been killed!" He exploded, his fury shooting up a notch as he thought of how close she and his sister had come to being shot.

There was a pause.

"I know. But I was thinking...how did he know I would be at my aunt's house? I had only just decided to go there half an hour before we arrived. And we told no one where we were going. Not even your mom knew. Nor Dan. He's really mad at me about that, by the way." Dan's deep voice agreed in the background. "But my point is, that shooter— he shouldn't have known."

Jace and Paul both nodded.

"And there's something else. I haven't told Dan this yet." Her voice lowered so no one could hear her. "Miles told us he was the one stalking me."

"What!" Jace, Paul and Dan all yelled.

"It's true. He was responsible for everything that was just threatening—the messages that told me to leave town, the phone calls, the pictures, the mannequin. And the snakes." She made a shuddering sound. "Not the shooting, though. Or the attacks on the jurors."

Jace was finding it difficult to process this new development. "Why?"

"Because Sylvie was his stepsister."

Whoa. He never saw that one coming.

"And Jace? He said Seth was her half brother. Same dad, different moms." She sighed. Jace wished he could be there with her, she sounded so sad. "What's going to happen to the poor kid? He was only trying to protect his stepmother from more pain."

"Melanie," Paul interrupted. "I understand that you feel for Miles. I do, as well. But Miles had a job to do. Not only has he shown exceptionally poor judgment by taking you ladies to an unprotected avenue, he has also broken the law and threatened those he swore to protect. I can't let that slide."

Her voice was subdued when she replied, "I understand. I'll stay with Dan until you come home, Jace."

Home to Mel. That was the best thing he'd heard all day.

Paul hit a button, severing the connection. Jace's mind flew back over the conversation.

"Bugs?"

Paul gave him a startled glance. "Jace?"

"Sorry, thinking about how the perp knew where they were going. There has to be at least one bug planted. That would explain the car showing up in Pittsburgh and outside the mall, as well as today."

"It would also explain how the perp knew when to plant that bomb in your car."

Jace rapped his knuckles on the window as he mused aloud. "I wonder if he knows where we are going now?"

"Probably not. We were outside, walking apart from the others when I gave you the warrant. We weren't in a vehicle or anywhere bug-able…"

"Excuse me, did you just say bug-able?" Jace sputtered.

"Yep, sure did. How else would you describe it?" Paul hit his blinker and made a swift left turn onto Maggie's street. "Anyway, like I was saying, I think we can assume our conversation when we decided to head out was private. It was totally random. My guess is that the bug is either in your mom's house or somehow in Melanie's possession."

Jace rubbed his jaw in thought. "I'll look into it as soon as we arrive home."

"Here we go." Paul cut the engine in front of Maggie's house and they exited the vehicle. "Let's do this."

They approached the steps from the left. As they moved in closer, Jace noticed the door was standing ajar. He silently pointed it out to Paul. In silent agreement, they pulled their service revolvers from their holsters. A loud crash came from inside the house. "In the back," Jace mouthed. Paul nodded. More crashing was heard inside. Whoever was in there was looking for something and seemed to be getting frustrated.

Carefully pushing the door open farther, they slid inside the house, keeping close to the walls. Paul moved around to the left, and Jace to the right. They met again near the hall and proceeded back.

Silence. Paul raised his hand and they stopped. There were two rooms ahead. Now that it was silent, it was hard to tell which room the noise had come from. Paul indicated that he would go to the room on the left, Jace would take the room on the right. Jace nodded.

He edged into the room, keeping his gun in front of him, sliding noiselessly along the wall. He darted glances to the right and left, but no one was in the room—or so it seemed. The intruder had definitely been in the room at some point, though. It had been trashed. Books thrown everywhere, papers scattered, glass and ceramic shattered on the floor.

Paul shouted from the other room, followed by a crash. Jace felt the floor shake.

He dashed toward the other room. A black-clad figure—a ninja?—ran into him at a full gallop, knocking him against a curio cabinet. It shuddered, and more glass shattered. Jace caught the ninja by the arm. The person twisted out of his grasp. Jace heard a sharp tearing sound as the fabric ripped at the shoulder. Still, the ninja managed to dash out the open kitchen door and yank it shut behind himself. By the time Jace managed to exit the door, the ninja was speeding away into the woods on a dirt bike. There was no way he could follow in the cruiser. Jace took off at run, but it was no use. The dirt bike grew smaller and smaller ahead of him as the perp put more distance between them. Finally, he was gone.

Remembering Paul, Jace ran back to the bedroom to find his chief rising out from under a bookcase.

"He toppled it over onto me." Paul shook his head. "I can't believe he managed to get away."

"Let's see what he was looking for."

An hour later Jace whistled. He had unearthed Maggie Slade's laptop computer. It had been sandwiched between blankets in a crate at the back of a closet. Not the place one would usually store such a device.

"She must have known she had something sensitive on that thing," Jace mused aloud.

"Let's open her up and find out what," Paul ordered, rubbing his hands together.

Soon they found emails and documents that put a whole new light on Sylvie's murder. For murder they now believed it to be. They just needed to connect the dots to find out who had committed it. Hopefully, they would also be able to find Maggie Slade, alive and well. Jace knew what they were both thinking, but not saying. Finding Maggie alive was growing less likely by the hour.

Melanie swung her legs back and forth like a kid as she sat in the chair Dan had provided for her at the police station. He was sitting behind his desk, diligently working on his reports. He never glanced her way. She suspected he was still mad at her over the morning's escapade. She wished he would say something, anything. It had been almost two hours since she had talked with Jace on the phone, and she was starting to go stir-crazy. What if something had happened to him?

She couldn't stop worrying over the fact that someone seemed to know each move they made. Her one comfort was that since she had no idea where Jace and Paul had gone, maybe the killer didn't know, either. After all, except for the incident when Jace was returning from Pittsburgh, she'd been present for every attack.

"Dan," she finally begged, hating the whining tone in her voice. "When will they be back? What if they're hurt?"

Dan reached for his coffee and took a sip, never removing his eyes from his computer screen. "I'm sure they're fine, Melanie. They'll call when they have news."

"Are you still mad at me?" Man, she sounded like a spoiled kid.

"Mad at you?" This time, Dan looked at her, startled. "Melanie, I was terrified that you and Irene might have been injured or worse, and furious at Miles for being so irresponsible. And I was a little irritated that you hadn't informed me of your plans. But I wasn't mad at you. Not exactly."

She didn't believe him. "We've been sitting here for two hours, and you haven't said a word to me."

Dan held up a finger, then riffled through the stack of paper on his desk until he found a notepad. He scribbled something rapidly, then handed it across to her.

She read the note to herself, eyes widening with each word.

Paul texted. Suspects bugs planted. Office and Tucker's place being searched now. Didn't want to worry you. Sorry.

She raised horrified eyes to his briefly, then wrote in reply:

Sorry for being a brat.

She leaned over and passed him the paper. He smiled and winked, then stood up. "I need to run this to Paul's secretary. Back in a sec." He strode from the room, leaving the door open.

After what seemed like forever, she heard Jace's voice in the hall. She jumped up and ran to the door of the office. Jace saw her and broke off what he had been saying to Paul. He strode to her and pulled her back into the office and shut the door before taking her in his arms. She rested her head against his chest and found comfort in the solid beat of his heart.

She could have gladly stayed like that for hours, but there were so many things to discuss. She raised her head, but when she looked at his face, the first thing she noticed was the weariness in the set of his mouth, the crease of his brow. She laid her hand against his cheek. He turned his head and kissed her palm. She sucked in a surprised breath. She couldn't say anything, though, because he bent his head and kissed her. It was a chaste kiss, but one that made her heart pound.

"Hey, don't let me disturb you."

Mel jumped back out of Jace's arms. She had been so wrapped up in him, she had noticed neither the opening of the door nor Dan's entry.

"Can it, Willis," Jace responded mildly. "It's been a harrowing day."

Dan smirked at his colleague. "The building's clear. No bugs found here. No word yet on your mother's house or Melanie's things. We should have that information in a few hours."

"Great. Paul and I found some—"

A knock stopped Jace in midsentence. A young clerk was standing in the doorway.

"Lieutenant Tucker, there's a young man here to see you. I put him in your office. He said to bring Miss Swanson with you."

"Really? Okay. Thanks, Sharon."

Dan circled Melanie and Jace to go back behind his desk. "I have some reports to finish up here. Call me when you're done. You can bring me up to speed then."

Jace nodded. He and Mel headed to his office. Mel froze in the doorway when she saw who was waiting for them. "Seth? What are you doing here?"

The young man who whirled to face them was a Seth she had never seen before. His cocky attitude was nowhere in sight. Anguish etched his face. He suddenly appeared to be older than his twenty-six years.

"Seth, what's wrong?" She hurried across the room to him. As she neared, Seth backed away from her, his hands warding her off.

"Don't hug me, Melly," Seth warned her, his voice hoarse. "I think when you hear what I have to say, you might hate me."

Mel blinked. What on earth? Hate Seth? She'd felt bitterness toward him and anger, but never hate. What could be so bad that she would hate the man she had once planned to marry? Whatever it was, she found she really had no desire to hear it. But she didn't have a choice at this point.

"Sit down, Travis." Jace closed the door and moved to sit behind the desk. He motioned for Mel and Seth to sit in the padded chairs across from him. Mel moved to a chair with leaden steps. Seth hesitated, then followed suit. Jace waited until they were both seated before speaking again.

"Okay. What's this about?"

"I think my father's the one who threatened the jurors," Seth burst out. "I think he's the reason Melanie went to jail."

"What—" A look from Jace stopped her.

"I'm listening, Travis. Explain," Jace ordered.

Agitated, Seth rose from the chair and started pacing the room.

"When that girl, Sylvie, was killed, it was close to the election. My father, he was feeling the heat from his opponent because I had been engaged to the lead suspect. Fraternizing with criminals and all that." Seth grimaced. "It didn't even matter that we'd already broken up and I'd left the country by then. He'd been after me for months to break it off with her. He threw her family history in my face. Said he wasn't going to lose the election because of the daughter of a drug-addicted wife beater."

Mel felt as if he'd punched her. Seth caught her glance, then looked away with a muttered apology.

"What makes you think he was responsible for the threats?"

"I'm an idiot. It never occurred to me to look into it further. He had coerced me into breaking it off with Mel. I figured I'd go along with it until the situation blew over and the election was finished. Then I'd get back with her, and things would be great."

Mel shook her head in disbelief. She wondered if she would have accepted him back, had things gone differently.

"I even told him that was my plan. He looked right at me and laughed in my face. Called me a fool. Said Mel was going down, and I needed to step back or she'd take me down with her. He was gleeful about it. I never thought about it at the time, but it was like he knew something. And this morning, I was working on his computer. He complained it was slow. I saw he had too much memory used. I noticed he deleted files, but never thought to empty his recycling bin. I doubt he even realized that those files were still on his computer." Seth pulled a paper out of his pocket. "I found this old email and printed it."

Seth handed a piece of paper to Jace.

Jace read it, his mouth tightening. He showed it to Mel. She gasped as she read an email telling the senator that "it has been taken care of. The Swanson girl won't be able to hurt your campaign again."

"I also have my suspicions that Dad has been cheating on my mom. His office staff love to gossip. Apparently,

Dad has received gifts from an unknown source. The day Mel went to jail, he received flowers. No card."

"Seth," Jace began, "what do you know about the young girl who was killed four years ago?"

Seth cocked his head. His forehead puckered. "What do you mean? She was a college student. That's all I know."

"You didn't know that she was your half sister?"

Seth staggered, the blood draining from his face. Mel had never seen him look so appalled. "No! What are you saying?"

Jace folded his hands on the desk. His face was blank, but compassion swam in his eyes. "It's true. Her stepbrother, Miles, confirmed it. And," Jace continued in a softer voice, "she wasn't the only out-of-wedlock child the senator had. I'm sorry to tell you this, but the Chief and I found evidence today that you have at least two other half sisters."

"I have sisters?" Seth rubbed his hands over his face and slumped in his chair. "I never knew anything about that, and I doubt my mom does, either. She's been really sick, and my dad doesn't like anything to upset her."

He raised his gaze to meet Jace's. "What are the odds that my ex-fiancée and a half sister I didn't even know I had would just happen to meet?"

"It's even worse than that, Seth. Like I said, you have two other half sisters. One of them is Maggie Slade. The missing juror."

SIXTEEN

A strained silence filled the room as Mel and Jace watched Seth struggle to come to terms with this new development. His jaw worked, and his hands clenched and unclenched. He fixed his eyes on a place above them. She knew the signs. He was close to his breaking point. Despite his betrayal, Mel found her heart wrenching at the pain in his eyes. The worst part was knowing there was nothing she could do to ease his suffering. So she stayed where she was, a silent observer.

"I have sisters," Seth finally whispered, his voice ragged. "I hope my father had nothing to do with Sylvie's death and Maggie's disappearance. I know he's obsessed with his career, but I really can't see him as a murderer—not of his own children."

"I hope you're right, Seth," Jace said. "But I have to investigate every angle. The chief has gone to bring your father in for questioning. We know he's involved somehow. When we searched her home, we found that Maggie's laptop was filled with research. Dates, at least one false marriage certificate, bank drafts. Probably bribes in return for silence."

"Did he—did my father know Sylvie was his daughter when she died?" Seth asked.

"I think so," Jace replied.

"Jace," Mel interjected quietly, "what about Maggie? Did she and Sylvie know each other? Did she know they were sisters at the time of the trial?"

It sounded so cold to ask about that, but she had to know. Did Maggie have an agenda at her trial? It seemed fishy that she would be picked as a juror.

"I doubt either one knew they were sisters. The evidence I collected at her house suggests that Maggie knew she was the senator's daughter. She was pretty bitter about it, too. She and Sylvie never had any direct contact as far as we could tell. Her notes said she had found the third sister, a kid of about thirteen now. She was emailing the girl's guardian. Her email logs show that last year, the guardian sent Maggie a picture of the kid—Carrie is her name, I think. Maggie noticed that she looked almost exactly like Sylvie. That's when she started to piece things together."

"It's quite a coincidence that Maggie ended up as a juror," Mel pointed out.

"Yeah, but I really think it was a coincidence." Jace stood and walked around the desk. He sat against the edge, stretching his long legs in front of him and folding his arms across his chest. "LaMar Pond is fairly rural. The jury was selected randomly."

Someone knocked on the door. A clerk stuck her head in. "Lieutenant Tucker, Chief Kennedy has returned with the senator. He wants you to join him in his office as soon as you are able."

"Gotcha. I'll be there right away."

Jace held out his hand to Seth. "I'll look into everything you've told us, Travis. You should probably scat before your dad sees you here."

"Yeah, you're probably right about that." Seth started for the door. He stopped and turned. "I hope you find whoever killed Sylvie, even if it's my dad. And I hope you find Maggie safe and sound. I always wanted a sister."

Melanie approached Jace, who was staring after Seth with a thoughtful frown. "Jace, I'm going to head off to the restroom for a few minutes. I don't really want to be in the room with the senator, either."

"Sure, Mel, that's probably a good idea. Just let me find someone to walk with you." She rolled her eyes at his paranoia, which he ignored. He stuck his head out the door and called for someone named Sheila. Sheila turned out to be a tall blonde in her forties. Her uniform was perfectly groomed from her shiny shoes to her ironed collar. Her hair was pulled back in a severe bun. She looked like a teenager's worst nightmare. Then she smiled, a big, open grin full of white teeth with dimples, and her whole countenance was transformed.

"Hey, Lieutenantt, what can I do for you?"

"Sheila, would you please escort Miss Swanson to the restroom?"

"Sure thing, my pleasure." Sheila flashed Mel another toothy grin and motioned her to come along. "We'll have to use the stairs. Maintenance is working on the elevator."

To her surprise, Mel found that Sheila was full of stories and mischief. She apparently knew just about everything and everyone from LaMar Pond. Mel enjoyed her conversation immensely. They had just reached the restroom when Sheila was paged. Uncertainty gathered on her face.

"Oh! I should call someone to stay—"

Mel shooed her away with a wave. "I'm at the restroom. I know my way back. Honestly, you go ahead. I'll be fine."

"You sure?" Sheila queried, already edging away.

"Yes, I'm sure."

Sheila sighed, her relief evident. "Great! I'll be back in just a minute—don't leave without me!" She dashed away.

Mel chuckled and entered the restroom. She just wanted a few minutes alone where she wouldn't run into the senator. Unfortunately for her, the restroom was already occupied. The woman at the sink sprayed herself liberally with perfume, then added a touch of hairspray to her hair.

Turning around in the entrance, Mel dashed out of the room. It was too late. The heavy, cloying perfume stuck to her clothes. She could already feel her air passages shrinking. A wheezing sound accompanied her breathing when she exhaled. Not a full-blown asthma attack, but it could turn into one. Sliding her hand into her pocket, Mel grasped her inhaler and used it. It was almost empty. She felt marginally better, but knew she needed her new one.

Sheila returned, a bright smile on her face as she noticed Mel sitting on a bench in the hall. It changed into concern when she noticed how Mel was breathing.

"Melanie, do you need help?"

"I need my new inhaler. Could you go to Lieutenant Tucker's office and get it out of my purse? I don't think I can do the stairs again without it."

"I don't want to leave you by yourself, though." Sheila gnawed at a fingernail.

"I'm in a police station. What could happen to me?"

Sheila seemed to come to a decision. "I'll be back in a jiffy." She dashed up the stairs, taking them two at a time. Mel watched her leave. She sat on the bench watching people pass. From where she sat, she had a clear view of the street outside.

A familiar form hurried past the police station. Cathy? Mel noticed that Cathy was looking upset. Her head kept swiveling back and forth, as if she was watching for something. Melanie grew concerned. Cathy looked as if she might need some help. Melanie shot a look back at the stairs. No sign of Sheila. Deciding she could wait a few minutes before she really needed her inhaler, she headed out the door after her friend.

Cathy headed past the post office, then turned into an alley. Picking up her pace, Melanie followed her. She found Cathy standing next to her car talking with someone who was sitting inside the vehicle.

"Cathy," Melanie called, a slight wheeze rattling out with each breath. "Are you okay? Do you need help?"

Melanie reached her friend's side and attempted a smile as she caught her breath. She moved her head to acknowledge the young man sitting in the car. He looked familiar. His dark hair was combed back, and he was wearing a suit and tie. She thought at first he was a young lawyer. Until she saw his eyes. His cold eyes that regarded her with contempt. Her smile froze and she began to back away.

"This is awkward, Mother," the man she knew as Dr. Ramirez said with a sneer. "Looks like we'll have company on our drive."

A hard object pressed against her side. Mel knew with stark clarity that what she felt was the barrel of a gun. Moving her head slightly, she found herself looking into Cathy Jordan's ice-filled eyes. She had no doubt the woman was capable of murder. The small click as Cathy cocked the gun gave her all the confirmation she needed.

Senator Travis was fuming. Jace couldn't care less. He'd been blustering for the past fifteen minutes about his ill treatment at the hands of LaMar Pond's incompetent police force. By unspoken agreement, Paul and Jace allowed the man to rant. When he seemed to run out of steam, Paul nonchalantly held up his arm so he had a good view of his wristwatch.

Jace bit back a grin. The senator swelled, looking

ready to explode. My, that couldn't be good for the blood pressure.

"I have half a mind to sue this office for harassment," the senator raged.

"By all means, call your lawyers," Paul advised, "We have a few things to clear up, and you might be needing them."

The legislator sneered. "What possible reason could I, a law-abiding citizen, have need of a lawyer? This is a witch hunt, and I won't stand for it."

"I don't know, Senator," Jace drawled, inspecting his hands. "It seems to me that bigamy is still illegal in the state of Pennsylvania. Isn't that right, Paul?"

"Last I checked it was," Paul confirmed.

"Bigamy?" Senator Travis repeated, losing some of his bravado. "I don't know what you're talking about. I'm a happily married man!"

"Twice!" Jace quipped. The senator glared. "We have a certificate, copied from the computer of Margaret Slade, of the marriage between yourself and her mother, Anna Slade. The curious thing is that the date indicates this marriage happened while you were already married to Mrs. Travis. Would you care to explain?"

The senator sat down in a chair, hard. "You can't understand."

Paul leaned forward, getting in the man's face. "Try me. We have several issues at hand, including murder. Start talking."

At the word *murder*, the senator's face blanched, and his hands trembled. Sweat pebbled on his protruding forehead. He took a handkerchief from his pocket and mopped his face and brow with it.

"Murder? No, I never killed anyone. You can't pin that charge on me. I did marry Anna. My wife and I were separated, and I didn't think we'd get back together. I figured I'd divorce her quietly, marry Anna and that would be the end of it."

"But you never divorced your wife," Jace stated, his voice hard.

The senator flinched. "No. She was diagnosed with a disorder of her nervous system years ago. She needed me. I left Anna and came home. Anna was very bitter. She was pregnant and couldn't collect support because I was already married. I paid her, anyway, and every month, she received money for Maggie's upkeep. In return, she promised to hold her tongue."

"Tell us about Sylvie," Paul ordered.

Senator Travis swallowed. "She was the product of a short-lived affair. I never knew about Sylvie until four and a half years ago. She started to dig into her parentage. When I found out I was her father, I tried to pay her off. I couldn't afford the scandal. And I didn't want Seth to know." He looked at them frantically, his eyes bulging as they darted between the two officers. "But I didn't kill her."

"Did you threaten the jurors into finding Melanie guilty?" Jace snarled. He was done playing games.

"No! Of course not. Why would I do that?"

Jace stalked over to the senator and glared down at him. "Because someone really wanted Melanie to go to jail. Someone threatened three jurors, then when two of them came forward, they were killed. Just like they killed Sarah Swanson. And now that same someone is after Melanie, and they apparently don't care how many people they kill to get to her."

Senator Travis leaped from his chair. He backed toward the wall, putting distance between himself and Jace. It was no use. Jace followed him like a hunter, never taking his furious gaze from the senator. The senator stopped when he came up against the wall. Jace was almost toe-to-toe with him.

"No! I didn't threaten or hurt anyone! All I wanted was to avoid the scandal and have an easy campaign."

The door to the office was flung open. A distressed Sheila barged into the room. She held Mel's inhaler in one hand, and her other fist was clenched around a small object.

"Chief! Lieutenant! Melanie's gone!"

"Gone!" Jace made an instinctive move toward the door to go find her, but Paul's hand on his shoulder forestalled him.

"Easy, Jace. Sheila. Tell us what happened."

"Yes, sir." Sheila sucked in a huge lungful of air. "I took her to the restroom. When she came out, her breathing was a little wheezy. She tried to use her inhaler, but it was empty. She asked me to come up and get this." She waved the inhaler she held at them. "I searched her purse and found this." Unclenching her fist, she held out the tiny object for them to inspect.

"The bug," Paul exclaimed.

"You say that was in her purse?" Jace questioned, urgency filling him.

She nodded. "I went back to find her and she was missing. I thought she might have gone outside. My daughter has asthma, and sometimes fresh air helps her. But when I went out, I couldn't find her."

"How long ago was this?" Paul strode away from his position near Jace and back to the phone on his desk.

"I don't know. Fifteen, maybe twenty minutes ago. She insisted she was fine. Sitting in a police station, what could happen?"

It took another fifteen minutes, but Paul was able to locate someone who had seen Melanie. A clerk who had been taking her break outside remembered seeing her walking down the sidewalk and turning into the alley. She hadn't thought anything of it, not realizing who Melanie was. A few minutes later, she had noticed Melanie in the back of a dark SUV leaving the station.

The driver had been a woman with bouncy blond hair. She recalled the vanity plate read CATHY7.

Cathy Jordan.

"I never even thought of Cathy!"

Paul picked up the phone and barked to the person on the other end that they needed all available personnel to search for the two women. He replaced the phone. "I never thought of her, either. It explains how she knew the jurors were coming forward—as Melanie's attorney, they probably contacted her directly. And if Melanie thinks of her as a friend—" he looked at Jace, who nodded his agreement "—that explains how she was able to slip the bug into place. But offhand, it's hard to come up with a reason why she'd want to hurt anyone—Sylvie, the jurors, Melanie."

"I know why."

Senator Travis. He'd forgotten all about the man. The senator had lost his arrogance. His shoulders slumped and his hands were slammed into his pockets. His eyes were a little wild-looking. Paul indicated he should continue.

"Cathy and I were involved years ago, back in North Carolina. When I broke it off to marry Helen, she was furious. Beyond furious. Crazy mad."

"How crazy?" Jace was putting two and two together. "Enough to stalk you? You said only personal items, items special to you, were taken when your home and office were robbed. Would Cathy have known they were special to you?"

"I don't know. Probably. But I do know one thing.

When Sylvie first started hounding me, Cathy was furious with me."

"Why?"

Head bowed, the senator confessed, "Because she had gotten pregnant when we were involved. Neither of us wanted a kid at the time, so she gave him up for adoption. Five years ago, he found her. Cathy felt I owed it to him to put him into my will, and she didn't want any other illegitimate children taking up any of what she saw as her share."

His eyes fell on a paper on Paul's desk. They widened. Pointing a shaking finger at the picture, the senator declared, "That's him. Why do you have his picture?"

Jace's blood ran cold. He was pointing to the sketch of Dr. Ramirez.

SEVENTEEN

They'd been driving forever. At least that's how it felt to Mel. Cathy had opened the backseat door for Mel, still holding a bright smile in place, and pushed the gun deeper into her side. "Get in," she'd grated between her teeth. Mel had gotten the message, and had forced her trembling legs to climb up into the SUV next to Dr. Ramirez.

He was not smiling. Quite the opposite. She shivered at the icy stare he kept trained on her. She squeezed up against the door in an effort to put as much distance between the two of them as possible. It was not far enough. With little effort, he reached out and grabbed hold of both her wrists in one large hand. With his other hand, he pulled out some rope and casually bound her hands together. Even more frightening was the utter lack of emotion with which he did this.

"Now, isn't this cozy?" Cathy smirked from the front seat, eyeing them through the rearview mirror. Her Southern accent had always seemed so charming and genteel. Now it just seemed sickening and fake.

At least Mel's breathing had improved. Walking out into the fresh March air, she felt her inflamed airways loosen enough so she was able to suck in almost a normal lungful of oxygen. She still heard her lungs wheeze when she exhaled. There was no way to fix that now. Her inhaler was back at the police station.

Jace. Surely he would start to wonder where she had gone. Hope struggled to breathe along with her weak lungs. Since her release, he had always come through for her. She hadn't thought she could count on any man…but she was beginning to count on him. She just needed to hang on and pray.

"It's such a shame this had to happen, Melanie. I really did like you," Cathy mused.

"Why are you doing this? I thought you were my friend?" Melanie wheezed.

Cathy laughed, and the hairs on Mel's arm raised on end. The sound slithered down her spine. "Friends? Oh, no, honey. You were a tool. A means to an end. And now I don't need you anymore. In fact, please excuse me for sounding callous, dear, but you're in my way."

"You're going to kill me, aren't you?" Mel lifted her chin. If she was going to die, she'd at least learn why first.

"Well, of course we are!" Cathy drawled. "Just as soon as we get to our destination. Isn't that right, James?"

James lifted one corner of his mouth in a semblance of a smile. It looked more like a snarl. "I don't know, Cathy. Asthma is often brought on by fear or stress. I suspect that if we do nothing more than torture her a little, her own lousy lungs'll do her in for us."

"He knows these things," Cathy confided to Mel. "He really did spend some time in medical school."

As if his knowing how to kill her was a good thing! *Stay calm Mel, stay calm.* Her lungs were feeling tighter.

"Why?" she managed to push the question through her stiff lips.

"It's the senator's fault, really." Cathy frowned, an ugly snarl darkening her face. "We were supposed to get married. Than he dumps me, leaves me pregnant and alone at seventeen. I had no choice but to give up my baby."

Cathy had been with Seth's father? Was that man capable of fidelity?

She focused in on Cathy's story. "But my son came looking for me." Cathy's eyes glowed. "Didn't you, James? We were all set to blackmail the senator for our share of his wealth. After all, I bore him a son before that wimp Helen. I'm far more fit as a wife for him than she is. His wife is sick, you know—some kind of degenerative disease. I've been dreaming for a long time of taking her place. I've even managed to get my hands on a few trinkets that should have been mine. Jewels, small heirlooms, things of that nature."

Something clicked in Mel's mind. She remembered the senator confronting Jace.

"You're the person who's been stealing from the senator," she wheezed.

"Stealing? Honey, once he marries me that stuff will be mine, anyway."

She was sitting with a madwoman. Only Cathy Jordan's eyes were totally sane. Obsessed, cruel, yes—but she was coldly sane.

"What about Sylvie? Did you kill Sylvie?"

Cathy lifted her chin and sneered at Mel in the mirror. "What a simpleton you are. Of course we did! That little snot came sniffing around the senator, too, claiming to be his daughter. Wanted him to acknowledge her, give her some money. Some of *my* money. I couldn't let that happen. Fortunately, James's adoptive father has connections. He learned very early how to survive, and made sure James got a good education. He was able to overpower Sylvie and drug her with enough bad heroin to kill her. But then you stuck your nose in where it didn't belong."

James broke into the narrative. "I saw you standing outside the dorm, watching me. I figured I'd take something of yours and leave it in Sylvie's dorm room to incriminate you, then make it look like you had killed yourself. Throw in a suicide note, and no one would be the wiser. Classic murder-suicide. Only someone came in and interrupted me before I could finish forcing the pills down your throat."

She had forgotten. One of her friends had been staying with her, helping with the rent once Seth had walked out on her. She remembered now that Alicia had been the one to find her.

"But why Aunt Sarah?" Melanie choked, her throat constricting, the back of her eyes stinging with unshed tears.

"I knew that juror had spoken to her. I'd gone through so much effort to threaten them, and she was going to tell. The idiot girl actually told me she'd been to see your aunt. She's to blame for both their deaths." Cathy pulled into a lane. It was nothing more than a tractor path, stretching far back into the trees. It curved around in front of a small hunting shack.

A shack that wasn't visible from the road.

Stepping from the car, Cathy hurried up the walkway to open the door and switch on a light. Melanie noticed that she was favoring her left wrist. James exited after her, walking at a leisurely pace around the SUV to open Mel's door. She attempted to scuttle across to the other side, away from him, but he seized her with a steel grip and hauled her from the car. Slamming the door behind her, he yanked her up the walk to join his mother. Mel fought with all she was worth, but her meager strength, diminished by her struggling lungs, was no match for his. He actually chuckled, as if amused by her antics. He dragged her inside and tied her to a wooden chair.

"It's ironic, isn't it, that I had decided to let you live?"

Cathy sashayed over to Mel and stood over her. "It wasn't until I realized that you and that detective were starting to figure things out that I started to worry. I heard you talking to your aunt at the hospital about the juror...I liked to go and visit Helen Travis, to make sure she was still weakening. I knew I had to act. It's a shame you didn't die when James tried to run you down that day. It would have looked like a hit-and-run. We had to resort to using the fire to try to make your death look like an accident."

"You're crazy," Mel breathed. "There was nothing accidental about the gun he shot at us. Or the car bomb."

"Yes, well, James got a little impatient. It doesn't matter. They can never trace that back to me. In fact, it actually helped me. I have airtight alibis for every instance."

"I'm hungry," James declared. "I say we let her sit and stew a bit before we finish her off. Who knows, maybe her asthma will get the best of her. Hopefully, no one noticed her following you. If we're lucky, maybe we can still pull her death off as an accident."

Cathy leaned over and patted Mel's cheek with her right hand. Mel recoiled. Cathy laughed. Mel could see it in her eyes, Cathy was just playing with her now. She had every intention of getting rid of Melanie.

Taking his mother's place, James leaned over to push his face close to Melanie's. The stench of stale cigarettes wafted from his clothes and his breath. Her stomach roiled. "You'd best say your prayers, little girl. You don't have much time left."

As the two sauntered from the room, James looked back over his shoulder with a malicious grin. He reached out and flicked a switch, turning off the single light in the room. Outside, it was still daylight, but inside the cramped little cabin with its dark paneled walls and curtained windows, it was nearly dark.

Melanie's imagination ran wild as the shadows played on the walls. Her breathing grew heavy and strained. Sweat ran down her neck. Unlike when she had been locked in the bathroom—was that really only days ago?—she knew who her tormentors were. And she knew their plans for her. She wanted Jace to come and find her, hold her and tell her he would protect her. Jace was probably in danger, too. Cathy and James both knew he was searching for the truth.

She bowed her head and prayed, silent tears running down her cheeks. She continued praying, even as her breathing grew more and more labored. She opened her mouth to suck in larger gulps of air, her breaths coming in harsh rasps. It felt as if someone were holding her bronchial tubes in the hands and squeezing them closed.

She was running out of time.

"Several people saw them in Cathy's black SUV," Paul informed the group of officers in the briefing room. "I'm passing around the license plate number, as well as pictures of Cathy Jordan and Melanie Swanson and the sketch of Cathy's son, James Sanchez. The suspects are armed and dangerous."

"Any idea where they're headed, Chief?" Dan Willis called out.

"We have several ideas." Jace picked up the remote control and switched the image on the screen to a new one downloaded minutes ago. "This is, of course, Sarah Swanson's house. Dylan and Scott will head there." Click. "This is the last known residence of Sanchez. Sheila and Sam, that's your destination." Click. "Dan, I want you to go with me to the hunting cabin owned by Cathy's brother." Click. Jace finished giving out the assignments, anxious to be on the way.

"Any questions?"

Seeing there were none, the officers departed.

Jace jogged to the stairwell and made it down the stairs in record time, Dan right behind him. Jace patted his uniform jacket. The inhaler was there, safe and sound. He only prayed he'd be able to deliver it to Mel.

Sliding into the new cruiser the department had just issued him that morning, Jace waited barely long enough for Dan to close his door before putting his foot to the gas pedal and roaring out of the parking lot. He flipped on his siren immediately. At his best guess, the cabin was twenty-five minutes away. Cathy and Mel had slipped out of the station forty minutes ago.

Jace had been all set to rush out at once, but Paul had convinced him to wait until they could get the information. No use driving around aimlessly.

Jace thought about all the new information they had gathered. He figured Cathy had put the bug into Mel's purse, but when? "It must have been at her aunt's house," he mused.

"What must have been at her aunt's house?"

"Huh?" Jace glanced over at Dan in confusion. The other man patiently repeated his question. "Oh, right. I was thinking. Mel had laughed about how klutzy Cathy was. How she had knocked over her purse at her aunt's house while Mel was packing her things to come to my mom's place. Didn't think anything of it at the time. Looking back, that must have been when she planted the bug."

"That would explain how Sanchez knew Melanie was going there after the funeral." Dan said, nodding slowly.

"It would also explain why Cathy was searching Maggie's house. I had mentioned in passing that I felt we'd find evidence there. She had to have known I had asked for a search warrant."

The radio crackled to life. Nothing found at Sanchez's old place.

Okay, there were still other venues to search. Jace felt his heart thud inside his chest. Why had he allowed the events of the past to have so much power over him? Melanie needed him. He knew she was suffering. Did she know he would search until he found her? She had to be terrified. What if—no! He would not think that. Melanie was fine. She was strong. She had survived four years in prison; she would get through this.

As soon as she was safe, he was going to beg her to give him a chance.

A second team called in. Still nothing. They were still fifteen minutes out from the cabin. He needed to pray. No words came to mind. He recited a Psalm in his head.

She had to be at the cabin. She just had to be.

When they arrived at the lane that served as a driveway, Jace cut the engine.

"Dan, you go up through those fields and creep around the back of the place. I'm going to head in from the side." Dan nodded.

As he neared the cabin, he could see that the curtains were drawn. He inched closer to the house, gun ready. He peered in through the sliver of open area between the curtain and the sill. Dining room. Empty. He edged around to the next room. Kitchen. Light spilled out from beneath the flimsy curtains. He could hear the low rumble of voices within. Cathy's high-pitched giggle was easy to pick out. A lower voice, a man's, was also distinguishable. He didn't hear a third. He continued around. The next room was dark. Instinctively, he ducked lower and tried to find a space to peer inside. He couldn't see a thing.

He hunched against the wall when the light flared on in the room. The sound of a slap was heard, and a cry. Melanie's. Relief nearly drowned him. She was alive. *Hold tight, Mel. I'll be there as soon as I can.* Quickly, he texted Paul. Mel at cabin. Call for backup & ambulance.

He edged back toward the kitchen. The light had been turned off. Dan joined him, having come around the other way. Placing his hand with care on the doorknob, Jace turned it a centimeter at a time. It was unlocked. The two officers managed to slide inside and approach the front room.

Cathy sat on the couch, legs crossed, watching serenely as Sanchez prepared a large needle. He held it upright and pushed the dispenser, getting rid of air bubbles and shooting out a few drops of liquid. He held the needle in his large hands and grinned at Melanie.

"I've always preferred to use chemicals. So much easier to cover your tracks. By the time they find you, it will look like you died from a fatal asthma attack."

He took a step closer to Mel. She used her feet to scoot the chair farther back, a whimper escaping her throat.

"Oh, you can't run from me, little girl." Sanchez chuckled, a truly malevolent sound.

"Hold it! Police!" Jace yelled. He trained his gun directly on Sanchez.

Cathy shrieked and flew at Jace, her long, manicured nails held out like claws. Dan stepped in front of her and grabbed her wrists. She howled as his hands closed around her injured wrist.

Ignoring the other officer as he cuffed the still-shrieking woman to a chair, Jace focused all of his attention on the man blocking his path to Mel. His chest constricted as he listened to her breathing rasp and wheeze.

James Sanchez flung himself at Jace, the needle in his hand poised to strike. Jace ducked under his arm and managed to knock the needle from his grasp. It skittered across the floor. The two men wrestled for control of the gun. Sanchez was larger than Jace, but Jace had desperation on his side. Mel needed him. And she needed the medicine he had in his pocket. He had to end this so he could go to her.

He managed get Sanchez into a wrestling hold. The other man was unable to move, but unfortunately, Jace couldn't release him to cuff him. Dan hurried over. James Sanchez was no match for two of LaMar Pond's finest. Dan removed Jace's handcuffs from his belt and snapped them on Sanchez. Jace left him seated on the floor while he sprinted across the room to Mel, the inhaler already in his hand.

"Okay, Melly. I'm here, honey. I have your inhaler. You're going to be fine." He held the canister to her lips. Fear trickled into his mind at their bluish tinge. He kept his voice steady with effort. "Okay, inhale, Melly." He paled as she tried to comply and broke off in a choking cough. "Okay, okay. Easy now. Try again."

She inhaled, but not deeply enough. Still, he thought he could hear a lessening of the wheezing.

Dan came to stand beside him. "Paul texted. The ambulance is five minutes out, maybe less."

"Thanks." Jace returned his attention to the woman before him. "Okay, honey, hang on with me. Five minutes. Then help will be here."

It was the longest five minutes of his life. He could hear the increasing shallowness in her breathing. He tried again with the inhaler, but her air passages were too inflamed to allow a deep enough inhale for it to work. Her complexion grew ashen and her lips turned bluer. She was fading right in front of his eyes.

"Mel, hold on, baby. Please stay with me."

He wasn't even sure she could hear him anymore; her eyes had started to glaze over.

When the paramedics rushed into the room, Jace jumped out of their way and let them take over. No one argued when Jace jumped into the back of the ambulance to ride to the hospital with Mel. He wouldn't have listened even if they had.

It was the smell she noticed first. The antiseptic smell that all hospitals shared, coupled with the woodsy after-shave smell she had grown to love so much. Jace was here.

Mel opened her eyes. She was in a hospital room with an IV sticking out of her left arm. A clamp on her finger was hooked up to a device that monitored her oxygen levels. What was the name of that thing? A pulse oximeter. That was it. Shifting her head to the right, she found Jace slumped in the chair beside her, apparently sleeping. His jaw was covered in stubble. How long had she been here? She looked down to see he was holding her hand even in his sleep. The sweetness of it had her catching her breath. At the sound, Jace's eyes flew open. He visibly relaxed when he saw she was awake.

"Thank you for coming after me," she whispered. It felt wonderful to be able to draw a full breath.

"I will always come for you," Jace promised her. He pushed himself out of his chair and leaned over to brush his lips across hers. They both smiled. Her eyes misted as she realized how close she had come to missing this.

"Melanie," he said, his voice hoarse, "I spent the entire night by your side. I asked God's forgiveness, and now I'm asking for yours."

She was confused. "Forgiveness? Jace, you saved my life. What do I need to forgive you for?"

"I let my past and my suspicious nature come between us. I nearly lost you. Mel, I was never as scared as when I couldn't help you yesterday."

She squeezed his hand, hard. "It helped having you there. I knew you would come for me. I knew you wouldn't let me down."

He squeezed her hand back. "Can I have a do-over, Mel? Without all the baggage and all the distrust? Because I don't want to walk away from what we have. I know it's happened fast, but I love you."

She pulled her hand from his so she could set it against his unshaven jaw. Joy and hope blossomed within her. She felt blessed. "Oh, Jace, I love you, too. Yes, of course, we can start over. This time, without someone trying to kill us."

"Maybe we could even go on a date, you know, like a normal couple?"

"Yes. I would love that."

He bent over her again and their lips touched. It felt like a promise of new beginnings.

EPILOGUE

Six months later

"We the jury find the defendant, Catherine Jordan, guilty of all charges."

Mel sagged against Jace's side. Jace slipped his arm around her shoulders, hugging her close to his body in silent support. Gratitude rose up in her for this man beside her.

It was over. Cathy had been found guilty. Mel had testified against her in court, her voice never wavering. She had also testified against James Sanchez earlier in the month. So had Jace, Dan, Paul and Seth. He was facing life in prison for the murders of Sylvie, Alayna Brown, Steven Scott and Aunt Sarah. Maggie Slade was still missing. The district attorney had decided not to charge the duo in connection with her case because he didn't have enough evidence. Recently, there had been a report that she had been seen alive near Pittsburgh, but that had not been proven. Jace and Mel still prayed daily for Maggie's safe return, and she suspected that Seth did, as well.

The judge pounded her gavel. Silence fell in the courtroom.

"Officers, please take Ms. Jordan into custody. Sentencing will take place one week from today." The judge removed her glasses and set them on the bench. Her kindly eyes caught sight of Mel. "Miss Swanson, on behalf of the Commonwealth of Pennsylvania, I offer my sincere apologies for the injustice that has been done to you. It is this court's decision that all prior judgments against you be revoked. All privileges accorded to law-abiding citizens are hereby reinstated."

"Thank you, Your Honor," Mel replied.

Jace squeezed her shoulder. She smiled up at him.

Mrs. Tucker and Irene were sitting in the row behind Jace and Mel. They leaned forward and gave her a hug. Mrs. Tucker and Mel had come a long way in the past six months. It was a pleasure now to spend time with Jace's mom. "Are you guys joining us for dinner tonight?"

"Yes, what time?" Irene looked distractedly at her watch. Mel knew she was supposed to pick up her sons from the babysitter at five. It was quarter till four now. Mel hurried to ease her friend's mind.

"Don't worry, 'Rene. We made the reservation for seven. That way, Paul and Dan will both be finished with their shifts. And Seth doesn't start until nine tonight, so he should have enough time to eat."

"Okay." Irene kissed Mel on the cheek, and then Jace. "I have Tony's mom coming to watch the kids. It's been a long time since Tony and I had a night out."

She waved as she departed with her mother.

"Let's go." Jace took Mel's hand and led her from the courtroom. Mel loved the feeling of his hand wrapped around hers. It was a common occurrence these days. He swung their arms between them as the automatic doors opened and they walked outside.

"There she is!"

Lights flashed and excited voices rose as reporters surrounded them. Mel stopped, a feeling of déjà vu hitting her. Jace tugged her hand, encouraging her to keep moving.

"Melanie! Are you bitter? What are your feelings today?" an eager reporter asked, getting within inches of her. Mel cast an anxious glance up at her sweetheart. Jace had slipped behind his cop mask again.

"No comment, people. Let us through."

"Jace," she tugged on his hand until he looked at her. "I want to give a brief statement."

Concern shone in his eyes. "Darling, are you sure? Don't feel you owe them anything."

"I'm sure. I'm through running."

Jace held up a hand. The reporters calmed, their faces alight with anticipation. "Miss Swanson will make a brief statement. Please don't hound her."

Mel stepped forward. The reporters all tipped their microphones in her direction. She kept her voice soft, making sure they had to be quiet to listen. "I want to tell you something. I went to jail for a crime I didn't commit, but I'm not bitter. I'm blessed. And I'm thankful for those who were willing to give me a chance, even though they thought I was guilty. I will pray every day for the families of the victims of Cathy Jordan and James Sanchez. Thank you."

Grasping Jace's hand again, she walked through the reporters, ignoring the questions they continued to shout out after her.

They stopped at Jace's new truck, and Jace opened the door for her. Before she stepped into it, he bent down a pressed his lips to hers. "I love you. You know that?"

"Yeah, I know. Love you back."

* * *

No words could describe how blessed Jace felt tonight. All the people he loved best were together in the private dining room at the local banquet hall. He had planned this get-together as soon as he knew Cathy's verdict would probably be decided today, so he could show his love and support to Mel no matter how the verdict went. Surrounded by his friends and family, and holding hands with the woman he adored, Jace was overcome by the emotion coursing through his veins.

He looked down at Mel. She was gorgeous tonight. Her emerald-green dress suited her perfectly. As did the diamond ring she was wearing. No one had noticed it yet. They had managed to keep the ring hidden by continuously holding hands or keeping her hand tucked in the folds of her dress. But it was time to let their loved ones in on the secret. Holding up his water glass, he tapped the side with a spoon. The others at the table settled and fastened their attention on him, their faces expectant.

In a single smooth motion, he stood and assisted Mel to her feet.

"I want to thank you all for coming. Tonight is a very special night. As you know, Cathy Jordan was convicted today." Applause rang from the group. He lifted Mel's hand and kissed her knuckles. Paul and Dan whistled. "More importantly, though, this wonderful, godly woman has agreed to marry me."

Mrs. Tucker cried out and ran to embrace the couple.

"I knew it!" Irene crowed to her husband.

Mel laughed, a full, rich sound that caught at Jace's heart. What had he done to deserve her?

"Paul, will you be my best man?"

Paul cleared his throat. "You know I will."

Mel looked at Irene, raised her eyebrows and said, "Well?"

Apparently, Irene had no trouble understanding this shorthand. She jumped to her feet and embraced Mel, jumping up and down at the same time. "Of course. You know what this means, right? Girlfriend, we are going shopping."

Mel giggled, then her face grew serious. Jace knew what was coming. They had discussed this, and both felt it was the best choice.

"Seth," Mel said in a husky voice. Seth grew very still. "You and I have been friends forever. I have no other family. Would you give me away? Please?"

Tears spurted to Seth's eyes. Looking around the table, Jace saw that he was not the only one in that condition. Seth rose awkwardly and made his way to Melanie. He hugged her, then shook Jace's hand.

In a voice that shook slightly, he replied, "I would be honored."

"I'd like to make a toast." Dan had risen. He held his soda aloft. "To Jace and Melanie. I'm glad to call you friends. I wish you a long life filled with love and laughter."

"Hear, hear!" Glasses clinked around the table.

Dan grinned. "I'm especially glad you decided to forgive my behavior when I first arrived, since as of yesterday, my transfer to the LaMar Pond Police Department is final."

"Good," Jace said with a grin. "Then I won't feel guilty when I take time off for my honeymoon."

Mel's arms crept around his waist. Joy filled his heart at he hugged the woman God had given him. He now understood. Love didn't take away from his ability to be a cop. Love gave him the ability to be the best cop, and the best man, that he was capable of being.

Jace bent his head and captured Melanie's lips in a sweet kiss. He smiled against her lips as the room exploded in cheers and clapping. He lifted his head and looked into her shining eyes. They had put the past behind, and were ready to take on their future. Together.

* * * * *

Dear Reader,

I hope you enjoyed Melanie and Jace's story. It was a joy to write their journey to overcome past hurts and prejudices and learn to trust enough to give love a chance. Even though LaMar Pond is a fictional place, it came alive for me as I wrote about Melanie and Jace.

Scripture tells us that everything has a season. I had always dreamed of being a writer. I put my dream aside to focus on raising my family. When my youngest started school, I began thinking seriously about writing again. I knew I needed to write inspirational stories. I had an idea about an innocent woman who went to jail and the cop who arrested her working together. It bounced around in my mind for months. When the editors for Love Inspired Suspense announced the Killer Voices Pitch contest, I decided to trust God and take a leap of faith. I will always remember the feeling when editor Elizabeth Mazer picked me to be on her team. When she called me to say she wanted my book, it was the realization of the dream God had put on my heart so many years before.

I have many stories in my mind that I am eager to write, but Jace and Mel will always hold a special place in my heart.

If you want to know more about what I'm working on now, you can find me at www.authordanarlynn.wordpress.com. I can also be found on Facebook and Twitter (@DanaRLynn).

Blessings,
Dana R. Lynn

REQUEST YOUR FREE BOOKS!

2 FREE RIVETING INSPIRATIONAL NOVELS
PLUS 2 FREE MYSTERY GIFTS

Love Inspired
SUSPENSE

YES! Please send me 2 FREE Love Inspired® Suspense novels and my 2 FREE
mystery gifts (gifts are worth about $10). After receiving them, if I don't wish to receive
any more books, I can return the shipping statement marked "cancel." If I don't cancel,
I will receive 4 brand-new novels every month and be billed just $4.74 per book in the
U.S. or $5.24 per book in Canada. That's a savings of at least 21% off the cover price.
It's quite a bargain! Shipping and handling is just 50¢ per book in the U.S. and 75¢ per
book in Canada.* I understand that accepting the 2 free books and gifts places me under
no obligation to buy anything. I can always return a shipment and cancel at any time.
Even if I never buy another book, the two free books and gifts are mine to keep forever.

123/323 IDN F5AC

Name	(PLEASE PRINT)	
Address		Apt. #
City	State/Prov.	Zip/Postal Code

Signature (if under 18, a parent or guardian must sign)

Mail to the **Harlequin® Reader Service:**
IN U.S.A.: P.O. Box 1867, Buffalo, NY 14240-1867
IN CANADA: P.O. Box 609, Fort Erie, Ontario L2A 5X3

**Are you a current subscriber to Love Inspired Suspense books
and want to receive the larger-print edition?
Call 1-800-873-8635 or visit www.ReaderService.com.**

* Terms and prices subject to change without notice. Prices do not include applicable
taxes. Sales tax applicable in N.Y. Canadian residents will be charged applicable taxes.
Offer not valid in Quebec. This offer is limited to one order per household. Not valid
for current subscribers to Love Inspired Suspense books. All orders subject to credit
approval. Credit or debit balances in a customer's account(s) may be offset by any other
outstanding balance owed by or to the customer. Please allow 4 to 6 weeks for delivery.
Offer available while quantities last.

Your Privacy—The Harlequin® Reader Service is committed to protecting your
privacy. Our Privacy Policy is available online at www.ReaderService.com or upon
request from the Harlequin Reader Service.
We make a portion of our mailing list available to reputable third parties that offer products
we believe may interest you. If you prefer that we not exchange your name with third
parties, or if you wish to clarify or modify your communication preferences, please visit
us at www.ReaderService.com/consumerschoice or write to us at Harlequin Reader
Service Preference Service, P.O. Box 9062, Buffalo, NY 14269. Include your complete
name and address.

LIS13R

SPECIAL EXCERPT FROM

Love Inspired
SUSPENSE

*Could veterinarian Jonas Parker give the Capitol
K-9 Unit team the break they've been looking for to
catch a killer?*

Read on for a sneak preview of
TRAIL OF EVIDENCE
by **Lynette Eason**,
the third book in the exciting
CAPITOL K-9 UNIT *miniseries.*

Brooke Clark jerked out of the light sleep she'd managed
to fall into sometime between her last sip of warm tea and
a prayer for divine help in solving her case. She rolled to
grab her phone from the end table. "'Lo?"

"I woke you up. I'm sorry."

Sleep fled. She sat up. "Jonas Parker?" Just saying his
name brought back a flood of memories. Both wonderful
and…painful. Along with boatloads of regret. The same
feelings that rushed through her every time she saw or
spoke to him. Amazing that she had no trouble pulling the
memory of his voice from the depths of her tired mind.
But then, why would she? She often dreamed of him,
their past times together. And they hadn't even dated. She
blinked. "What's wrong?"

"You're working the case about the congressman's
son's death, aren't you?"

"Yes. Michael Jeffries." Michael had been killed and
the congressman shot. The Capitol K-9 team was inves-

tigating. She cleared her throat. "You called me at four o'clock in the morning to ask that?"

"No, I think I found something that you might need for your investigation."

"What?"

"A phone with a picture of Rosa Gomez and her two-year-old son as the wallpaper."

Fully awake now, Brooke swung her legs over the edge of the bed. At the foot of the bed, her golden retriever, Mercy, lifted her head and perked her ears. Rosa Gomez, the congressman's housekeeper, had been found dead at the bottom of the cliffs in President's Park. The Capitol K-9 team was also investigating her death due to the connection between her and the congressman. "Where did you find the phone?" she asked.

The fact that Rosa's wallet and phone hadn't been found with her body had raised a lot of questions. Like had her fall from the cliffs been an accident, or murder? If it had been an accident, where were the items? And if it had been murder, had the murderer stolen them?

"Ah...well, that's the problem. And one of the reasons I called you."

"Come on, Jonas, tell me."

"I found the phone under my son's mattress."

Don't miss
TRAIL OF EVIDENCE by Lynette Eason,
available May 2015 wherever
Love Inspired® Suspense books and ebooks are sold.

SPECIAL EXCERPT FROM

Love Inspired.

When the truth comes to light about Oregon Jeffries's
daughter, will Duke Martin ever be the same again?

Read on for a sneak preview of
THE RANCHER TAKES A BRIDE,
the next book in
Brenda Minton's
miniseries MARTIN'S CROSSING.

"So, Oregon Jeffries. Tell me everything," Duke said.

"I think you know."

"Enlighten me."

"When I first came to Martin's Crossing, I thought
you'd recognize me. But you didn't. I was just the mother
of the girl who swept the porch of your diner. You didn't
remember me." She shrugged, waiting for him to say
something.

He shook his head. "I'm afraid to admit I have a few
blank spots in my memory. You probably know that
already."

"It's become clear since I got to town and you didn't
recognize me."

"Or my daughter?"

His words froze her heart. Oregon trembled and she
didn't want to be weak. Not today. Today she needed
strength and the truth. Some people thought the truth
could set her free. She worried it would only mean losing
her daughter to this man who had already made himself

a hero to Lilly.

"She's my daughter." He repeated it again, his voice soft with wonder.

"Yes, she's your daughter," she whispered.

"Why didn't you try to contact me?" He sat down, stretching his long legs in front of him. "Did you think I wouldn't want to know?"

"I heard from friends that you had an alcohol problem. And then I found out you joined the army. Duke, I was used to my mother hooking up with men who were abusive and alcoholic. I didn't want that for my daughter."

"You should have told me," Duke stormed in a quiet voice. Looks could be deceiving. He looked like Goliath. But beneath his large exterior, he was good and kind.

"You've been in town over a year. You should have told me sooner," he repeated.

"Maybe I should have, but I needed to know you, to be sure about you before I put you in my daughter's life."

"You kept her from me," he said in a quieter voice.

"I was eighteen and alone and making stupid decisions. And now I'm a mom who has to make sure her daughter isn't going to be hurt."

He studied her for a few seconds. "Why did you change your mind and decide to bring her to Martin's Crossing?"

"I knew she needed you."

Don't miss
THE RANCHER TAKES A BRIDE
by Brenda Minton,
available May 2015 wherever
Love Inspired® books and ebooks are sold.

SPECIAL EXCERPT FROM

Love Inspired HISTORICAL

Emma Hewitt has a groom waiting for her in Oregon,
but will she fall for handsome, brooding loner
Nathan Reed during the journey instead?

Read on for a sneak preview of
Lacy Williams's
WAGON TRAIN SWEETHEART,
the exciting continuation of the series
JOURNEY WEST.

Emma went looking for Nathan.

He stood in the shadows behind the wagon. Alone, just
as he'd been since he'd come into their caravan to drive for
the Binghams. He watched her approach without speaking.

But there was something in the expression on his face.
A wish…

Maybe the same wish that was in her heart.

Stunned that he'd allowed her to see it, he who was usually so closed off, she swallowed hard.

"I need you, Nathan," she said softly, reaching out a hand
for him.

He jolted, as if her words had physically touched him.

"The children are restless. Come and tell a story. Please.
At least until supper."

And he came.

He settled near the fire, but far enough away to be out of
her way. His surprise was evident in the vulnerable cast of
his expression when Sam crawled into his lap and rested his

back against Nathan's chest.

As she worked with Millie to cook the stew and some pan biscuits, he told of tracking a cougar on a weeklong hunt. Of the winter that another trapper had stolen furs out of Nathan's traps until he'd figured out what was happening. Of losing a favorite horse and having to pack out a season's worth of furs by himself.

"Your beau is so brave, going on so many adventures," Millie said softly at one point, as they began ladling the stew into bowls for the children. "And not bad to look at, either."

Emma looked up to find Nathan's eyes on her. Had he heard Millie? She couldn't tell.

She didn't think quite the same about Nathan's stories of life in the wilderness. Each adventure sounded...*lonely*. His stories reflected that he was alone most of the time.

The isolation would have driven her crazy, she was sure. Not having someone to talk to, to listen to her joys and sorrows...

She regretted the resentment she'd held for her siblings over the trip West. She'd been at fault for not expressing her fears and desire to stay back home. She was thankful she'd come, or she never would have faced her fears.

But more than that, she wanted to give that to Nathan. Family.

Would he let her? Would he let her in?

Don't miss
WAGON TRAIN SWEETHEART
by Lacy Williams,
available May 2015 wherever
Love Inspired® Historical books and ebooks are sold.